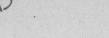

GUARD

He did not know of Michigan Hole, none to tell him that the road agent hideout was almost directly to the west and that there were trails to bring riders to this grassy valley. He had only intuition to serve him, but when the first rifle spoke, it was almost as though he'd expected the attack.

But that was only the beginning.

Fifty yards above, a rifle spun a red blossom against the night. Thorson brought his gun arcing up, triggering at that brief brightness.

Then rifles were speaking everywhere, and six-shooters too, a half a hundred guns divided between one hillside and the other, catching the treasure train in a withering crossfire. . . .

Also by Norman A. Fox

Thorson
of
Thunder Gulch

NORMAN A. FOX

A DELL BOOK

Published by
Dell Publishing
a division of
Bantam Doubleday Dell Publishing Group, Inc.
1540 Broadway
New York, New York 10036

The trademark Dell® is registered in the U.S. Patent and Trademark Office.

ISBN: 0-440-21061-5

Printed in the United States of America

Published simultaneously in Canada

June 1995

10 9 8 7 6 5 4 3 2 1

OPM

To Elmer and Ann

Chapter One
THE ROAD TO EL DORADO

They were two. They had put a boulder between themselves and the wind, for this was a high place, the backbone of a continent, the region where the waters divided to run their erratic way to separate seas, and the summer never came here and the air was wine and the snow eternal, a mottled pattern of slaty whiteness against the gray of rock and the dun drabness of stunted trees.

They had waited here a long time, and a litter of half-smoked cigarettes testified to the impatience of their vigil. From the talus slope where they made their stand, they could see a stretch of the stage road, a muddy ribbon that climbed to the crest of the divide just below them, then dropped down the western slant of the pass until it was lost in a tangle of treetops and the haze of distance.

They were big men, both of them. Blanket mackinaws and weathered sombreros and colorless mufflers made them alike, but their similarity was more than a matter of garb or breadth of muscle and bone and was fashioned from an elemental savagery that gave them kinship to each other and to this sprawling, primitive land. The one had a shock of shaggy hair and a broad and ponderous face with a tiny, crescent-shaped scar at the tip of his left cheekbone. It was he who said, "Late! That stage is at least three hours late. Come sundown, I hightail it. The scalp of no one man is worth a night atop the Wolverine."

The other drew a long and thoughtful puff on a cigarette which had burned short enough to stain his fingers. "Even if it comes, what makes you so sure it will stop?" he asked. "Let's get down there where the sight of a gun will do some good."

"You ever climb the slant of the Wolverine?" the scar-faced man said derisively. "Try it and you'll rest your hoss a good many minutes at the top. And if you've got six of 'em, and a heavy Concord behind, you'll rest that much longer. They'll stop, Lonny. Don't worry about that."

But this Lonny was a man unconvinced, and he knew a gnawing need for action, for his were the ways of violence and all else was beyond his understanding. Impatience had made him petulant. "Granting they do stop," he argued. "How you gonna know this Thorson if he's aboard? You said you'd never seen him."

"I'll know him," the scar-faced man said with that same easy assurance. "Ever see a picture of a Viking, Lonny? Big broad-shouldered galoots they were, with yeller hair flowing down their backs, and eyes as blue and cold as the seas they sailed. That's the kind of gent Thorson will be. Big as Matthew Fee, or bigger. A Scandihoovian giant and a first-class fighting man. And when the minute comes that we sight him, we'll get this business finished fast. I know the Thorson breed. Don't let him get a gun out from under his coat."

"Listen!" said Lonny. "They're coming."

Borne on that toothy wind was the clatter of wheels over a rocky, rutted road, the faint pistol-like explosion of a driver's whip, the creaking of leather thoroughbraces and the jingle of harness chains. And that medley of sound drew all the slackness out of these two men, leaving them taut. Each pulled his muffler up over his nose and looked to the loads of his gun, and they were standing straight and expectant when the stage topped the rise and wheezed to a stop. The driver wrapped his reins around the brake lever, the coach door bulged outward and the passengers spilled stiffly into view. "See?" the scar-faced man said triumphantly. "It's a chance to stretch their legs, and I knew they'd take it! This'll be easier than shooting fish in a rain barrel!"

But now the skepticism of Lonny had something tangible to fasten onto. "Where's your yeller-haired giant?" he demanded. "Look, there's a woman aboard. And a dark-haired dude that doesn't stack up to giant-size. And a drummer, and that tall gent with a muffler around his face. Mister, this is a wild-goose chase!"

Only the eyes of the scar-faced man were exposed now, and they were puckered with puzzlement. "Thorson came to Fort Benton a week ago," he said flatly. "His name was on the passenger list of the *Prairie Queen*, and his name was on a hotel register in town. I know, because I talked to a man who saw it and half-killed a horse to carry the word back to Matt Fee. Even if Thorson had business to keep him in Benton for a few days, he'd have to be on this stage unless he wanted to wait another week. Me, I'm having a look at the jigger with his face wrapped up!"

He raised his gun and sighted along it carefully and pressed trigger. The mountains caught the thundering echo and multiplied it, toying with it among the peaks, and a gout of dirt upheaved at the feet of the passengers as the two men came charging down the slope. . . .

Some came questing for gold by way of the river, journeying by steam packet for a month and more, following the Big Muddy from St. Louis to the Port of Fort Benton, head of navigation on the upper Missouri. Some took the overland trail north from the Mormon stronghold of Salt Lake. But all these, the Argonauts and the leeches who followed in their wake, came to a crossing of the trails at sprawling

Shoshone at the foot of Wolverine Pass. Here the stage road forked, and here the wanderers by water and the wanderers by land changed coaches, catching the ancient Concord that plied weekly between Shoshone and the fabulous new diggings of Thunder Gulch, over beyond the Wolverines. Thus Shoshone had become the meeting place of wayfarers headed for a common destination and varied destinies.

One such man, hauled from Fort Benton and left to sit, had cooled his heels in the Shoshone station for all of three hours; a summer cloudburst had blocked the road to the south and the Salt Lake stage was long overdue. He was a man who lacked four inches of being six feet tall, a dark-haired, blue-eyed man in his mid-twenties. A tailored, knee-length plantation-style coat fitted him well, his pantaloons were gray and of fine texture, but there was a touch of foppishness in his pearly double-breasted waistcoat and the rakish angle of his tall beaver hat.

Against the long delay, as against all the exigencies of frontier travel, he had put a practiced patience, but it had about run out when the Salt Lake stage, mud-spattered, rolled into town. There were three passengers aboard it—a moon-faced drummer, a woman, and a tall man, muffled to the eyebrows in spite of the heat of the day. Their luggage was stowed atop the Thunder Gulch stage while they bolted a meal, and Josh Hoskins, grayed veteran of many a mountain run and smelling eternally of horses, was on his perch when the four lined up before the station. To each he gave a speculating glance, and to the young man he said, "Up here, if you like."

And because Tod Thorson knew that this was an honor bestowed only upon men of apparent merit, he bowed gravely, held open the door of the coach for the woman and the others, then set his foot upon a hub and clambered up beside Hoskins.

Then they were clattering out of Shoshone, the little settlement falling away on the flats behind them, and Josh Hoskins sent his six horses straining against the harness as though he were possessed of a deep and compelling need to recapture those three lost hours. In the wild rush of that ride, with trees and rocks blurring past, there was no chance for talk; a man would go hoarse pitting his voice against the thunder of hoofs, the monotonous clacking of the sand-boxes over the wheels.

By three o'clock of that afternoon they were toiling up the slant of the Wolverine, and at this crawling pace Hoskins separated and re-separated the ribbons impatiently and said, with a trace of irritation, "She'll be midnight and past afore we come rollin' into Thunder Gulch. How can a man keep a schedule when he had to wait on idjits that take three hours to dig out of a bit o' mud?"

"I'm anxious to see the town," said Thorson.

"She's booming. And she's something for the eye. She's Alder Gulch and Bannack and Last Chance all rolled into one, and Frisco in '49 couldn't tie her in some ways. You'll like her, stranger. And you'll hate her too, and you'll wonder why you ever came to such a gawd-forgotten place, and you'll never leave till they fold her up and give her over to the ghosts."

"Eden and El Dorado," Thorson murmured. "Gomorrah and Gehenna and the Promised Land rolled into one!" But he could see that his remark held no meaning for Hoskins, and he said, "Tell me more."

"She grew out of nothing," Hoskins said. "When Lars Thorson planted his pick in the original discovery claim, he planted the seed that blossomed into Thunder Gulch. Two years ago she was a ragged tent, a-flapping in the wind. Today she's a town. And another two years'll give her back to the ghosts."

"That's twice you've said that," Thorson observed. "What makes you think Thunder Gulch will be so short-lived?"

"There's men as makes a town, and men as breaks 'em. Lars Thorson made Thunder Gulch. He planted the seed and he nourished it, and he wanted something lasting to come of it. It was him fetched in a newspaper editor and a parson and started building a school. It was him who was the first marshal of the diggings, and they'll never have a better. Ah, he was a man, Lars Thorson, big and broad-shouldered and yeller-haired. A Viking, the *Thunder Gulch Trumpet* called him. But he's dead now, died from pneumonia after battling his way over the pass for grub for the camp when she was blizzard-locked and starving last winter. And who's to stop Matthew Fee?"

"Matthew Fee?"

"He's the other kind, the man who breaks a town. I've seen his breed in all the diggings, wringing the last ounce of dust out of the earth, packing it in their pokes and going their way. Lars Thorson could see a tomorrow, a day when the gold bubble busted but Thunder Gulch would still be standing, a day when a railroad would run over Wolverine Pass and they'd take timber out of the hills and cattle out of the grassy valleys. But Matt Fee don't care for the tomorrows. It's today he wants to hold in his hand."

"What's his business?"

"He's got his Hurdy-Gurdy House and his games and his rotten likker. And what gold dust comes out of other claims goes over his bars and tables. And them that comes at his beck and call reap their share too. It's murder and robbery on the trails and in the town. It's bad traveling and worse luck for the honest, and no end to an evil beginning. It was a black, black day for Thunder Gulch when Lars Thorson died. They needed vigilantes in California and in the Alder Gulch diggin's here in Montana, and they got 'em. But who's to stand up against Matthew Fee and bring law to Thunder Gulch? Who, I ask you?"

To all this Tod Thorson gave his grave and solemn consideration, studying these facts as a man might study a hand of cards when the ante is high and the game is at its crisis. And so lost was he in his own reflections that the stage lurched to a stop at a swing station where they'd change horses before he realized they'd been approaching it.

"Carrying anything in the treasure boot?" he asked when the switch was made.

"My extra socks and a bottle against the miseries that wet weather brings," said Hoskins. "Treasure goes *out* of Thunder Gulch, not into it. Though it's little gold that's being moved these days with the road agents on the prowl."

"I see," said Thorson and smiled. "Then you won't be needing a man at shotgun, and I'll sit inside for a while."

None of the passengers cared to ride backwards, Thorson discovered, for all three were huddled in the one seat, and Thorson placed himself across from them and matched their silence for many a rumbling mile. Then he stirred faintly and dipped his hand into his inner coat pocket for a cigar case, this slight movement revealing, for a fleeting moment, the black butt of a Colt's forty-five in a shoulder holster nestled under his left armpit. He snapped open the cigar case, glanced at the woman and said, "Do you mind?"

"Not at all," she replied and smiled as though she found amusement in the notion that she might have minded.

Thorson extended the case toward the muffled man, who said, "No, thank you. I use them at times, but I'm afraid I'd find no enjoyment in anything at the moment." He flicked long fingers toward his face. "Neuralgia," he explained. "Traveling always brings on an attack."

The drummer also declined, and Thorson got a cigar aglow and settled back in the seat and fell to studying his fellow passengers anew. From buttoned shoes to a stiff derby, the drummer looked like a hundred others Thorson had seen, and there was little of the other man to be inventoried since his face was effectively masked. He was long and thin, this muffled man, and folded in many places to accommodate himself to the seat. The woman was the most interesting of the trio.

She would never see forty again, Thorson decided, yet where other women had used artifices to ward off the years, she had defeated time by the simple expedient of ignoring it. This he knew with no consciousness of how he came by his knowledge. She had a face that was handsome rather than pretty and her hair was dark brown, well combed and piled high, and about her there was an air of breeding that was linked to an air of resourcefulness. He sensed that she had lived fully and without compromise, and he wondered what brought her to Thunder Gulch and how she would fit into that brawling boom-camp. And his curiosity was great enough that he asked, "This your first trip to the diggings, ma'am?"

"Why, yes," she said. "Are you acquainted there?"

"In a way," he said. "I've never been across the Wolverines, but I've connections in the gulch."

"Then perhaps you know Jamieson Hazzard," she said. "I am affianced to him. My name is Belle Kincaid. We plan to be married as soon as I arrive."

The muffled man stirred quickly. "Jamieson Hazzard! Miss Kincaid, Hazzard is as good a friend as

I've ever had. And of course I know your name!
Many's the time I've heard him speak of you."

And because Tod Thorson also knew the name of
Jamieson Hazzard, he looked from one of these people to the other and prepared to speak. But suddenly they were all aware that the stage had stopped
again, and a glance from the window told Thorson
why. "We're at the crest of the divide," he announced. "The driver will want to rest his horses.
Come, it's a fine chance to stretch ourselves, folks."

Swinging the door outward, he came to the
ground, giving his hand to Belle Kincaid, and the
muffled man and the drummer piled down after
them. "It's cold," the woman said and shivered, and
the tall man drew his muffler tighter, and Thorson
started to ask them whether they'd rather wait inside the Concord. He was speaking when the dirt
spurted near his boot toe and the gun boomed on
the slant above, and he raised his eyes to see the two
mackinaw-clad figures bounding down upon them.

"Road agents!" Josh Hoskins cried and stretched
his hands high.

What Tod Thorson did then was mostly instinc-
tive. His cue was to hoist his hands, for the loss of
his few valuables would be little enough if his life
were spared. Yet much of that grim talk he'd had
with Josh Hoskins on the lower slant still shadowed
his mind, and it was thus that he sensed that it was
more than watches and wallets these road agents
sought. "Treasure goes *out* of Thunder Gulch, not
into it," Hoskins had said. What dark and sinister
purpose, then, had kept these masked men waiting
at the crest of the divide?

Thorson raised his hands only to the level of his
shoulders, and then he put his right hand inside his
coat, and when it whisked out again he was holding
the Colt's forty-five and triggering it. Those two
were halfway down the slope now, firing as they

came, and from the corner of his eye Thorson saw the muffled man drag Belle Kincaid to the ground.

Then one of the road agents was having trouble with his legs, for they had become hopelessly tangled, and he went down on his face and slithered half the length of himself before he lay still.

The other road agent had flung down behind a heap of talus, but this scanty shelter served him not at all as Thorson drove three quick slugs in his direction. Josh Hoskins had lowered his hands and was fighting his rearing horses, and Thorson's tall beaver sat at an even more rakish angle, bored through by a bullet. But the second road agent, the scar-faced man, was clutching his left side, cursing stridently and making a wild run for the cover of a man-sized boulder.

Holding his gun poised, Thorson watched the man dart from one boulder to another, and he waited for a fair shot and found no opportunity. He sprinted forward himself then, but his quarry had rounded the shoulder of the slope and Thorson proceeded warily, fearful of an ambush, until he heard the quick beat of retreating hoofs and knew that his man was upon a horse and fleeing.

Thorson walked back toward the stagecoach. The drummer and the muffled man each had Belle Kincaid by an elbow, and Josh Hoskins was down off his perch and had turned the fallen road agent over. The rocks had done him a lot of damage, and, in answer to Thorson's pointed look, Hoskins shrugged and said, "The gulch is full of faces. I've seen 'em all; I've seen none of 'em. Even if this one was in shape for a look-see, I couldn't be sure."

The muffled man came forward. "I'm a doctor, but not of medicine. Yet I know a little of healing. Perhaps—"

"Not him," Thorson said. "Not even if you were the best doctor in the world."

The drummer produced a frilly handkerchief and touched it to his sopping forehead and eased the bite of his celluloid collar with his finger. Fear made his voice shaky. "Murder!" he said. "That's what they had on their minds! It grows worse each day. As sure as my name's Ed Folinsbee, I'll stay in Thunder Gulch no longer than it takes to call on my trade. Do you understand me, gentlemen!"

Josh Hoskins looked at the dead man. "Another delay!" he grumbled. "We'll have to heap rocks on him since you couldn't budge the ground here-abouts with blasting powder!"

And when the stage rumbled down the western slant of Wolverine Pass, a mound of rocks marked the place where it had stopped. And Tod Thorson had forgotten the things he might have said to Belle Kincaid, fiancée of his friend, and he rode beside Josh Hoskins once again, keeping his gun ready and his eyes wary. This, then, he thought, was the road to El Dorado, and death had waited along its reaches to greet him.

Thunder Gulch was beyond, and the night would bring him to it, and he wondered what would be the end to such a beginning.

Chapter Two
DEATH COMES AT DAWN

On mornings like this, Virginia Drew found it good to be alive, for the thin sunlight gave a different hue to all it touched, and even Thunder Gulch lost the veneer of its sordidness under such a wand. She could see most of the camp from the doorway of her cabin, the twisted gulch with its double row of shacks and false fronts and tents, the slopes on either hand and the buildings that had crawled up their rocky sides as though to put themselves beyond the contaminating touch of the town proper. And because hers were eyes designed for dreaming, she could look upon the camp when the day was new and see it as the town it would someday be.

Once she'd sworn she'd heard a meadow lark at such a dawn. But the stamp mill that Matthew Fee had freighted over the rough trails had made its ceaseless thunder for many a week now, and when she'd told her breathless tale of music in the morning to Jamieson Hazzard, he'd patted her hand and smiled his wry smile and mumbled something about her working too hard.

She came down the gulch this day, as she did every day, a trim, erect figure in calico, her bonnet dangling in her hand, carried against the hour when the sun would grow pitiless. Her eyes were hazel and she had a shimmering wealth of honey-colored hair, yet she wasn't a pretty girl. Her nose had a turn to the end of it, and her mouth was a mite too wide, but many a man in the diggings had looked at her and remembered dreams long discarded.

She had a wholesomeness to her, and an inner

warmth, and she had brightened everything she'd touched.

The camp was already teeming with life as she walked along. High-sided freight wagons crowded the dusty way, and there was a litter of lighter vehicles—buggies, surreys, buckboards, pack trains— and the cursing of drivers who tried to find a way through all this confusion made a discordant medley, jumbled and meaningless. To one side of the road, a man who'd spent the night at drinking had perched an empty whiskey bottle upon a rock, and he stood at a distance from it and drove bullets at the bottle, sighting with a great show of deliberation, but missing his target each time. Then she came to the first of the strewn planks that served for sidewalks, and she moved through a motley assortment of humanity, rough-clad and well-clad, bestowing her nod and her smile upon all she knew, quickening her pace past the flamboyant front of Matthew Fee's Hurdy-Gurdy House and coming at last to the log structure that bore the sign:

THUNDER GULCH TRUMPET—JAMIESON HAZZARD, EDITOR AND PROPRIETOR.

The door was locked and she searched her reticule for a key and let herself into the ink-and-glue– pervaded atmosphere of the tiny office to the front of the building. Two doors gave off this room, one leading into the press room, the other into Jamieson Hazzard's cramped living quarters. He was all the father she'd ever known, and he owned as much of her heart as her real father would have, but she was a woman now so the two of them had bowed to propriety and taken separate lodgings. She tapped on Hazzard's door and said softly, "Pi . . . ?" When there was no answer, she stepped inside, grimaced at his unmade bed and the general disorderliness of the room and set to work tidying up.

This done, she came back into the office, rolled up

the top of the battered desk and found the latest
copy of the *Thunder Gulch Trumpet*. And because
there was only this one issue of the edition that had
clanked off the press last evening, she knew that
Jamieson Hazzard was already out distributing his
paper.

She knew every word of that paper, for she'd set a
great deal of it herself while Hazzard had paced the
length of the press room, dictating at a furious rate.
She'd proofed it and dummied the various items
into place and taken her turn at the handle of the
old press. But she snuggled into a chair, becoming a
minute dab of color in this drab room with its filing
cases, its potbellied stove and print-littered walls,
and turned to the editorial page where a boldface
caption carried the title: THE DEVIL AND RORY
O'DOONE, and she read the editorial beneath it:

With the miner's court sitting in session this afternoon to select a new town marshal for Thunder
Gulch, it is an hour when the voters should seri-
ously view the candidates who aspire to that office. Since your editor is one of them, any remarks about his qualifications would naturally be
colored—and consequently worthless. Thus it is
more than mere modesty that mutes the *Trumpet*
on this score.

On the other hand, we ask you to scan the
doubtful merits of the opposition's nominee. Consider, then, Rory O'Doone who toils not, neither
does he spin, yet Solomon in all his glory was less
opulent than the loudmouthed Rory. From
whence comes the gold dust that he spreads with
such a lavish hand across the bars and gaming
tables of our more nefarious establishments?
Even Rory, deep in his cups and at his loudest, is
silent on that subject.

Is he the man to fill the boots of Lars Thorson,

first marshal of Thunder Gulch? The answer is obvious. Will he even compare to the man who succeeded Lars Thorson and who held the office until his untimely demise a week ago, passing away, oddly enough and violently enough, in the alley behind the Hurdy-Gurdy House? Again the answer is obvious.

Lest these seeds fall upon rocky soil, let us have a simple summing up. Is a vote for Rory O'Doone a vote for law and order? Or is a vote for this strutting braggart actually one for that devil who stands behind him—that devil who is Matthew Fee?

Think it over!

She put the paper aside as a shadow moved swiftly across the desk, for Jamieson Hazzard had come bustling into the office.

"Morning, Ginny," he said and kissed her quickly.

"Morning, Pi. You're trying to look careless, which means you're bursting with news. Out with it."

Dignity had always rested awkwardly on the rounded shoulders of Jamieson Hazzard. He affected a cutaway coat and a flowing tie, but no matter how white a shirt might be when he donned it, he was sure to have it smudged with ink before an hour ran out. Scarcely taller than Ginny Drew, who stood five feet four, he was turning bald at the crown and the temples. He was the symbol of all his harried breed, the frontier newspaperman, progressive and profane, a crusty crusader whose torch burned fitfully against the winds of chance. Smiling wryly, he said, "We called off our vigil an hour too early last night, Ginny. The stage rolled in around midnight. They were slowed up in Shoshone, and again at the top of the Wolverine."

She came quickly to her feet. "And *he* was on it?"

"Yes," Hazzard said. "He's over at the Empire House; his name's on the register, big as life—Dr. Huntley Drew. Your father is here, Ginny. And that same stage brought J. Todhunter Thorson. And Belle Kincaid!"

She said, "Then it's a big day for you, too!" And was glad.

"It would be a big day if only Huntley Drew had come. I haven't seen him yet. He'd want his sleep this morning, I knew, if he came bumping down off the Wolverine at midnight. Besides, I thought you'd like to be the first to see him."

She thought about that for most of a minute. "No, you must be first," she said. "But what about Belle Kincaid?"

"I asked for her," he confessed. "She's still sleeping, Ginny. Do you know, I'm almost afraid—"

She looked into his face and saw what the years had done to it, sagging his jowls and etching lines into the healthy pinkness of it, and because she was a woman and knew the nature of his fear, she laughed. "She's afraid, too," she said assuredly. "She's wondering what *you*'ll see when you face her. And none of that counts, Pi. The important thing is that you've both found out the truth after a long, long time."

He sighed. "I was to write the big book of the day and set the world on fire," he said. "She had her career too; a thousand audiences were to applaud her. That's what we chose instead of each other. And this is what I've gotten." The sweep of his arm took in the littered office. "Her dreams burned down to ashes too, and what of the years we tossed away? Ginny, when your chance at happiness comes, take it at once and hold it tightly in both your hands!"

"She's here now," Virginia said softly. "She's here, and everything else is behind you. You'll make a handsome bridegroom, Pi. And I'll try to catch the bride's bouquet."

He held silent for a while, and she could hear the steady beat of a distant gun, and she remembered the drunken man who was trying to smash a whiskey bottle. Hazzard shook himself like a man awakening from a long sleep, and he said, "It's a big day for both of us, and for Thunder Gulch. Young Thorson will make a stir hereabouts, or I'm no judge of the breed. Yet—*J. Todhunter?* Does that sound like the cub of old Lars? But we'll have a look at the Viking before the day is through, I'll wager. And meantime I'll call on Dr. Huntley Drew."

"You'll . . . you'll try and tell him what I'm like, make it easier. It will be so strange. . . ."

He cupped one of her hands in his. "I know, dear," he said. "You *are* strangers to each other, aren't you. But he's your father, Ginny, and blood is thick. And you can be proud of him, very proud. He's a great and good man, dear. In archeology his name and Dr. Wish's stand among the highest. They spent their lives poking into the hidden places, but Huntley Drew's no squint-eyed scientist. Did I ever tell you that he was one of the spirits and brains behind the organizing of the vigilantes in the California diggings? And he'll bring a new day to Thunder Gulch, too. I'm not half afraid of being marshal here with two such men as Huntley Drew and the son of Lars Thorson to back me."

"If I'd only seen him once in a while through the years," she murmured.

"He had his work to do, and it called him to places where he couldn't take a child," Hazzard said. "I'm proud that he gave me the responsibility of rearing you, Ginny. At the beginning, I thought there'd be Belle to help me with the task. But I've done well for an old bachelor. I think Huntley will agree."

He turned toward the door, and she followed after him and adjusted his tie and brushed the brown specks from his coat lapels. He had an addiction for snuff, and she'd fought a long and futile fight against it. "You'll stop in and see her too, if she's awake," Ginny said. "Try not to stuff your handkerchief into your coat pocket; it makes such a horrid bulge. And don't get your hair all mussed up by running your hand through it."

"I'll try," he said forlornly.

"And, Pi—be careful," she added. "I've just reread that editorial about Rory O'Doone. Matthew Fee will have read it too, by now. I've jumped at every shadow since Zeke Lockhart forced the nomination on you a week ago. You mustn't take chances, Pi."

"I've watched my back," he said. "Now there'll be others to do it for me. I said it was a great day for Thunder Gulch. There'll be a stir in this camp when I introduce a pair of my friends at the miners' court election this afternoon!"

Then he was gone, and in her mind's eye Ginny Drew followed him across the dusty street and up the plank walks to the Empire House and to the room where her father would be waiting. And the picture she conjured quickened her nerves until she wandered restlessly about the room, picking up many objects and putting them down without being aware that she'd held them.

From a litter of books atop the rolltop desk, she took a ponderous volume with a gold-stamped backbone bearing the title: MAYAN CIVILIZATION—A LINK BETWEEN THE NEW WORLD AND THE OLD? She ran her fingers across the names of its authors—Huntley Drew and Absalom Wish, then thumbed through the thin, closely printed pages, reading snatches here and there, trying to piece together the personality of Huntley Drew, stranger and father to her, from this dry and learned tome. Then she resolutely put the book aside and, with a quirk of her shoulders, marched into the press room and went to work. This had always been soothing medicine when there was waiting to do and the minutes dragged.

The forms of yesterday's edition of the weekly *Trumpet* lay on the press, and she unlocked them and began nimbly to re-sort the type, dropping each slug into the proper case. She was adept at this task from long practice, but once she bruised her finger and used a word she hadn't learned at the select girls' school to which Jamieson Hazzard had sent her in her teens. She toiled on, and the morning sun wasn't much more than perched above Wolverine Peak when she'd finished. She washed her hands then, and came into the office and stared through the window at the knot of men coming toward the building, stared without seeing them until she realized who was in their midst and what this coming portended.

Afterwards she was to wonder if she'd heard the gun, but no matter how many times she turned this morning over in her mind, she was never to be sure. Guns were part and parcel of Thunder Gulch in this, its lawless stage, and the barking of them went as unnoticed as the barking of dogs. And there'd been that man who was so intent on demolishing a whiskey bottle. Yet there'd been another gun, and it had done its work, and Jamieson Hazzard was being carried back to his office, bloody and inert and horribly still.

She knew he was dead. She knew it before they carried him through the doorway and laid him on a table, for the grave solemnity of their faces gave mute testimony that there was nothing more to be done for him. She wondered if she were going to faint, and wished that she could, and she put out her hand toward the table. She saw the tall, scholarly-faced man with the gray-sprinkled modified Imperial, and even before he came and put his arms about her, she sensed that he was Dr. Huntley Drew. She saw the other stranger too, the dark-haired dandified young man with the bullet hole through his tall beaver. Dr. Drew was saying, "There, there, dear. It's a hard blow, I realize. You must brace yourself. . . ."

A miner, one of the group who'd toted Jamieson Hazzard home, cursed in a monotonous voice and made no apology for it. "Shot down right in the middle of the street," he said. "Shot down with dozens around him. There'll still be an election, I suppose, but Rory O'Doone's won without a vote being cast! This is Matt Fee's day to laugh, damn him."

She heard him, and she knew what he implied, but it didn't matter to her. Not then. For in this, the moment of her greatest grief, the time of parting from the one who'd walked with her always, she seemed queerly detached from herself. And her sorrow, oddly enough, was not for the man who lay dead, but for Belle Kincaid, who had come upon a troublous journey and who would find tragedy instead of happiness at the long trail's ending.

Chapter Three
THE DEVIL AND RORY O'DOONE

Tod Thorson had bedded at the Empire House because it was the handiest hotel from the stage depot and because Josh Hoskins, tooling his Concord into the gulch after midnight, had recommended the place—with certain reservations. "She's got no more bedbugs than anywheres else you might bunk," Hoskins had said. "And there's less shootin' in the hallway at the Empire." Thorson had been so weary that he'd have settled for a hayloft; the woman, Belle Kincaid, was reeling on her feet when they unloaded; the muffled man, Dr. Drew, was walking stiffly; and the drummer, Ed Folinsbee, was tired enough that he'd forgotten his terror of this camp. Each went to an assigned room with no more than a good-night nod to the others.

The Empire was one of Thunder Gulch's more pretentious establishments, a two-storied affair and only recently built. Thorson's room was graced with a carpet that had lost its color, a bed that had stood much abuse, a bureau, listing badly to the left, and a cracked pitcher and bowl which perched precariously atop that scarred monstrosity. Also, there was a chair. To Thorson's surprise, he discovered it to be a claw-and-ball–footed Chippendale, much older than himself.

A kerosene lamp swung overhead, but Thorson didn't bother to light it. He undressed slowly, listening to the throb and roar of sleepless Thunder Gulch around him, and he planted the chair against the door and placed the pitcher and bowl upon it, mindful that today had seen one attempt at murder. His name was on the hotel register now, and any man could find him, but forcing into this room would be another matter.

His simple precaution taken, he laid his gun on the floor beside the bed, within easy reach of his fingers, then wormed himself into the blankets. He spent a moment savoring the blissful flow of weariness that permeated him, and he fell asleep in the midst of that moment.

The first light, filtering through the window, awoke him, and a quick glance gave assurance that his crude burglar alarm was as he'd left it. He lay in bed for a long time, contemplating the ceiling and turning many things over in his mind, then he dressed, put the room to rights and got himself hot water for shaving, a ritual he was forced to perform without a mirror. Then he left his room in search of breakfast.

The Empire House had a dining room of sorts, adjacent to the horsehair sofa- and cuspidor-strewn lobby, and in the dining room Thorson found a secluded table and listened, in lieu of a menu, to a slatternly woman's brief accountal of the offerings. When the meal was brought to him, a copy of this morning's *Thunder Gulch Trumpet* was dropped on his table, and he raised his black brows at this unexpected courtesy. He saw the name of Jamieson Hazzard on the sheet's masthead, and it brought a smile from him and he began reading. At that precise moment, Jamieson Hazzard was crossing the lobby to climb to Dr. Drew's room, and by this narrow margin did Tod Thorson miss seeing the man alive.

The editorial, THE DEVIL AND RORY O'DOONE, won Thorson's attention, and he read it carefully, the mention of Matthew Fee's name bringing a quick reminder of the things Josh Hoskins had said yesterday. He put the paper aside and ate thoughtfully, and when he'd finished he picked up the sheet again and diligently read every word of its copy. Paying his bill and wincing at the boom-camp price, he strolled into the lobby and over to the desk. His own name was there on the register, and below it came Belle Kincaid's and Ed Folinsbee's and the flowing signature of the muffled man—Dr. Huntley Drew, San Francisco.

Tod Thorson looked at that name for all of ten seconds, whistled softly and turned toward the stairs. But before he'd mounted half a dozen steps, Dr. Drew brushed past him, hurrying downward.

"They shot him!" the man cried wildly. "They shot him down, out there in the middle of the street! I saw it happen from my window—saw him fall!"

It was Tod Thorson's first real look at Dr. Huntley Drew. The man still wore his muffler, but it was knotted loosely about his neck and his gray Imperial was tangled in it. His was a scholarly face, thin-lipped and ascetic, and there was much in the look of him to make him a man worth remembering. But no part of his wild babbling had any meaning for Thorson, so he set his hand firmly on the tall man's arm and said:

"Who? Who was shot down?"

"Hazzard—Jamieson Hazzard! Ten minutes ago we were shaking hands in my room, and he was leaving to fetch my daughter to me. And now they've killed him!"

"*God!*" Thorson said and went down the stairs as though he'd been catapulted, Dr. Drew panting at his side. And they came together into the street and to the growing knot of men who were gathering, and they elbowed ruthlessly among these men until they stood looking down at the sprawled and silent figure at their feet.

"He's dead," someone said needlessly.

"Give us a hand," Thorson ordered and knelt to lift Hazzard's head into his arms.

Thus they came carrying their lifeless burden,

Thorson and Dr. Drew and a ready group of volun-
teers, and they brought him into the *Trumpet* office,
guided by one who knew the way, and Thorson saw
the girl and saw Dr. Drew go to her and put his
arms around her and say something that was lost
upon Thorson, for shock had numbed him. A miner
spoke up too, and then the girl said dazedly,
"There's a woman over at the Empire House. Belle
Kincaid. She'll want to know . . ."

Thorson was nearest the door, and he slipped outside and crossed obliquely over to the Empire
House, taking his time in going, for this was a task
to no man's liking. Into the hotel, he scrutinized the
register again and mounted the stairs.

He came to the door bearing the number he
sought, and he drummed his knuckles upon the
door and heard a voice say, faintly, "Come in."
When he entered a room not unlike his own, Belle
Kincaid was sitting on the edge of her bed, a robe
thrown over her nightgown, and because she was
immeasurably older than she'd been, he guessed
that the news had preceded him.

"You've heard?" he asked.

She nodded numbly. "They were shouting it from
door to door down the hall a moment ago," she
said.

That left him with his task performed, and he
fumbled for words and finally said, "I'm Tod Thorson. He was my friend and my father's friend. I
want you to know that. And I'll never leave this
town till I've found the man who killed him. I want
you to know that, too."

She said, "That won't bring him back to life."

He nodded, closing the door softly behind him,
for he understood her need to be alone.

He went down the stairs and to the street again,
and, across the way, he saw the high figure of Dr.
Drew and he strode over to the man.

"I thought you'd be with the girl," Thorson said.

"She'll need me, but not till later," Drew said. "Right now she's better off alone. There's an undertaker of sorts here, and I've just spoken to him and made all the arrangements that are necessary. Poor Jamieson! And poor Virginia."

He shook his head, then thrust out his hand. "I saw your name on the register this morning, Thorson. Too bad the truth didn't come out yesterday when we were riding together. There is so much we might have discussed, but I was a sick man. I'm Dr. Drew."

"I know," Thorson said, taking the proffered hand. "I flattered myself that those two road agents were after *me* atop the Wolverine. But if they could have known I was coming, they could have likewise been expecting you. I suspect that your record with the California vigilantes isn't unknown in these Montana diggings."

Dr. Drew sighed. "That was a long time ago. I supposed it was a turbulent page from my past that would never be re-opened. But there's a need for us here, Thorson. That's plain enough. And it seems we're partners, at any rate."

Thorson shrugged. "I haven't had time to look into affairs," he said. "I was in St. Louis when Jamieson Hazzard wrote that Lars was dead. Hazzard said that you staked Lars for the trip that brought him to this gulch and to the strike that made this town, and that the original discovery claim was in Lars' name and yours. It's been years since I last saw Lars Thorson, and more years since I saw Hazzard or you. I knew, of course, that Hazzard had raised your daughter. It's a black day for her."

Dr. Drew said, "Lars Thorson could make a fortune or lose one faster than any man I ever knew. Yes, I staked him when he came to Montana, and I was to have half of all he found—or so he insisted.

But you know that Lars Thorson really owed me nothing."

"I know he saved your life once—in the Sierras. But if he had you as a partner in this deal, then you and I are the co-owners of the discovery claim."

"Shall we go and have a look at it?"

"Later," Thorson said. "There's something more important to me at the moment. The town elects a marshal this afternoon. Hazzard was a nominee; so is some fellow named Rory O'Doone. Hazzard's paper tells it that electing O'Doone would be the same as electing a certain Matthew Fee—and he's the man behind all that's wrong in Thunder Gulch, according to what I've heard. Hazzard obviously had the same opinion, and Hazzard was so close to the truth that he's dead today. I'd like to be at that election, Doctor."

"And so would I," said Drew.

They found Virginia Drew dry-eyed when the pair of them came to the *Trumpet* office as the sun stood high. Hazzard's body had been removed, but when Thorson saw the stricken look of the girl, he knew that each familiar thing in this room was reminding her of the man. Dr. Drew broke an awkward silence by speaking swiftly. "We'll have a lot of talking to do, my dear," he said. "A pair of lifetimes to go over, in fact. But all that can wait. We've come to ask you if you feel up to attending the election today. We'd like someone with us who knows the gulch and its people. But . . . ah, excuse my oversight. Virginia, this is Tod Thorson."

At least that brought her out of her apathy. *"Him?"* she said.

"I know," Thorson said. "You expected another yellow-haired giant like Lars Thorson. Everybody does. A black Viking is something that just isn't in the cards. But it happens that my mother was a dark-haired Irish girl who could walk under Lars Thorson's outstretched arm. Yet they tell it that when she was heavy with me, she took a rifle and stood off a horde of claim-jumpers in the California diggings—and dusted three of them for keeps."

Ginny said, "I'm sorry. I didn't mean to be rude."

His smile was quick and warm. "Maybe I'm too touchy. But it's a bother, being only half big enough to fill my father's boots. Will you go to the election with us?"

"And see the triumph of Matthew Fee?" she asked wanly. "Why not? Pi would be there . . . if he could."

They made aimless small talk until a bell began to boom in the distance, and Ginny nodded then and they went out of the office, the girl locking it behind them. They followed the strewn planks to where the buildings thinned, then turned to their right and climbed a zigzagging path which led toward a huge, barnlike structure far up the gulch's slant. A bell surmounted this building, and it tolled steadily, a tocsin that drew many men up the trail, singly and in groups. Clinging to a shoulder of the slope, at a distance, stood an immense stone house, remote and aloof, and Ginny said, "That was Lars Thorson's. You'll be living there, I suppose."

But Tod said quickly, "That man up ahead! The one with the red sash! Who is he?"

She raised her eyes, her lips tightening. "That," she said, "is Rory O'Doone."

He studied the broad back of Rory O'Doone, but he gave no indication of what had aroused his interest in the man, and he watched O'Doone until the fellow bobbed into the meeting hall above. When the three of them also entered the building, Thorson blinked from the sudden change to semidarkness, seeing dimly the huge room with its raised platform at the farther end, the planks stretched from barrel to barrel, from packing box to packing box, and the scattering of men who filled these rough seats. Huddled to the back of the room were a few Chinese, and Thorson stared at them in surprise as he seated himself.

"They work such diggings as have been abandoned by the miners," Ginny explained. "They have no vote here, but they naturally have an interest in what goes on in the gulch. Poor devils, they've suffered as much as anybody from the road agent curse."

Thorson was looking for Rory O'Doone again, and he found him easily enough. O'Doone was sitting farther to the front, and on the other side of the aisle that ran down the middle of the room. The man wore miner's garb, but his clothes were extremely colorful, and they'd never been sullied by the dirt of the diggings. Red-topped boots and crimson sash and silver-inlaid bowie knife made Rory O'Doone a sight for the eyes. He was in his element here, was O'Doone, greeting friends boisterously, ignoring the studied frowns of the better element, a man self-assured and confident. His was a broad and ponderous face, topped by shaggy hair, and there was a tiny, crescent-shaped scar at the tip of his left cheekbone. But that had no meaning for Tod Thorson, who'd never before seen the face of Rory O'Doone.

Yet his eyes clung long and thoughtfully to Matthew Fee's candidate for town marshal, and he remembered the man climbing the trail to the meeting hall, and he remembered a masked, mackinaw-clad man who'd bent in like fashion as he darted from boulder to boulder atop Wolverine Pass, a man who'd clutched his left side, seared by Thorson's lead.

"He's got both friends and enemies here," Thorson whispered to Ginny. "I can see that. How do they stack up, one against the other?"

"About half and half," she decided after a moment's appraisal. "Look, Zeke Lockhart's climbing the platform to bring the meeting to order. He's head of the miners' court."

Thorson looked at the thin, gentle-eyed, gray-haired man who stood upon the platform, and decided that Zeke Lockhart didn't have the stuff of martyrs. He said, "Why hasn't your miners' court stomped out the road agents?" And he anticipated Ginny's answer before she said bitterly, "What good is a watchdog without teeth?"

Lockhart's raised hands were silencing the shuffling of boots, the gruff rumble of voices. "The meeting's in order," he announced. "There's no point in wasting time on formality. Every man jack of us knows that Pi Hazzard was killed today. That makes only one candidate for marshal, unless somebody does some more nominating . . ."

"Matthew Fee?" Thorson whispered quickly. "Is he here?"

"I've looked for him," Ginny said. "No, he isn't wasting his time on a pat hand."

"I'm waiting for nominations," Lockhart continued. "Come on, gents. Speak up."

Again there was the furtive slither of boot soles, the restless creak of benches. All this endured for a minute's span, then Rory O'Doone stood up, all smiles. He raised his arms, and Thorson was quick to note that he hoisted the right one abruptly but he handled his left more gingerly. "Seeing as there's no opposition," said O'Doone, "I reckon it's unanimous, and there's no sense voting. All I gotta say is that I'm gonna make you the best damn' marshal these diggings have ever had. And the drinks are on me down at Matt Fee's Hurdy-Gurdy House."

Tod Thorson came to his feet. "I'm a stranger

here," he said loudly. "Mr. Chairman, will you tell me what qualifications a candidate must have?"

"Why, there ain't nothing much to it," said the astonished Lockhart. "You have to be a resident of Thunder Gulch, and your record's got to be clear. We couldn't elect a peace officer who'd ever been mixed in anything crooked."

"Then," said Thorson, "I'm afraid Mr. O'Doone doesn't qualify. He and another stopped Josh Hoskins' stage on Wolverine Pass yesterday. I know. I was on the stage. The man's a road agent!"

Rory O'Doone personified the surprise of all these men, and he swung his head quicker than the rest, gaping at Thorson with both astonishment and hostility. "And just who in hell are you, mister?" he demanded. "And where's your proof for what you just said?"

"The name doesn't matter," Thorson countered. "I'm asking you to strip off your shirt, O'Doone. I'll bet this bullet-plugged beaver that you've got your left ribs bandaged."

"This jigger's trying to make a joke outa our election!" O'Doone roared. "If I undress right here just to prove him a liar, I'm going to be hoorawed for it from here on out!"

"Don't let him make a fool outa you, Rory!" someone shouted, and others raised their voices to back the man. "We ain't listening to no dude!" one cried. Thus did O'Doone's followers identify themselves, and Thorson was quick to note the number. Also he was quick to do some thinking. From the first, he'd had only a suspicion to prompt him, a suspicion born of that faint similarity between Rory O'Doone climbing the slope to this building and Rory O'Doone scuttling to shelter on another slope, far up on the Wolverine. But a suspicion, without proof to back it, was worthless as the whisper of the wind, so Thorson said, desperately, "O'Doone, your

friend of yesterday had a few words to say before he
died. Shall I tell this court what they were?"

It was sheer bluff, and it wrung a startled gasp
from Dr. Drew, but its effect upon Rory O'Doone
was even more electrifying. He dropped his hand to
the gun in his belt, and he said, "Damn you, mister;
you won't be as lucky as you were yesterday!"

But Zeke Lockhart, by some legerdemain, had
also produced a gun, and Thorson revised his original estimate of the man as he saw that movement.
"There'll be no shooting in here, O'Doone!" Lockhart thundered. "Not unless you want to stop the
first slug! You've just admitted that you saw this
stranger yesterday. So I'm asking for a look at your
side to see if it's bandaged like he says!"

A score of men were suddenly on their feet, their
mingled voices making an incoherent medley,
throaty and menacing. Some were friends of
O'Doone's; some foes, and Thorson could sense the
tension in them and was possessed of the queer feeling that he could put out his hand and touch the hot
and ragged edges of their tempers. Even the Chinese to the rear of the room had taken to chattering
shrilly. If Rory O'Doone had owned the true quality
of leadership, this moment might have been his, for
his followers were many and in a mood for violence.
But O'Doone began shouldering his way toward the
door, and a press of men moved to block him.

"You've showed him up for what he is!" Ginny
said, and Thorson found her standing at his side.
"You've finished him in Thunder Gulch!"

Then he felt her fingers tighten spasmodically
upon his arm, and he saw men suddenly stand
rooted who'd been pushing and jostling a moment
before. He didn't guess what had put this restraint
upon them, for he hadn't heard the door creak
open. But he heard the name that burst from a
dozen lips, and he heard it carry across this room

like a ripple spreading over the disturbed stillness of
a deep pool. And thus, even before he turned his
head for a look, he knew that Matthew Fee had
come.

Chapter Four
MARSHAL OF THUNDER GULCH

Matthew Fee was big, much bigger than Thorson had expected him to be. The man stood over six feet, and his sweep of shoulders might have belonged to a blacksmith. He dressed well, his taste running to dark broadcloth and a show of jewelry, and his suit was carefully cut and of good texture, but the coat sleeves bulged tightly with the flow of muscle. There was strength in his face too, and he would have been strikingly handsome except for a dross of flesh that made his features ponderous. He was excessively florid and carried an air of good humor as though it were his stock in trade. Smiling as he came up the aisle, he said, "Gentlemen! What's the cause of all the commotion? I could hear you halfway up the hill!"

Every man looked to his neighbor to make reply, and Zeke Lockhart became suddenly and painfully aware of his position here. He cleared his throat twice, then said, "O'Doone's been accused of road agenting. He's just the same as admitted that it's true."

The good humor faded from Fee's face as though a lamp had been extinguished behind his heavy-lidded eyes. "Who says so?" he demanded.

"I do," said Thorson.

Fee gave him no more than half a look and was patently unimpressed. "I don't seem to place you," he said.

"The name is Thorson. J. Todhunter Thorson. I'm new here."

It was the second time a name rippled across that room, but Thorson found no satisfaction in that

whispered acclamation, for this was like sitting on a
powder keg when the fuse has burned down out of
sight. Ginny still stood beside him and, without taking his eyes from Fee, he reached and forced her
down to the bench and moved slightly to put her
behind him. His thought was that Fee made a vast
and eye-filling target, and he knew where he'd place
his first shot if Fee's coming here made a showdown
between one element and another. But Matthew Fee
only gave him a longer look and said, "Well, well!
Any kin to Lars Thorson?"

"His son. It's hard to believe, isn't it?"

"Yes and no," Fee countered. "Since Lars cashed
in his chips and left the discovery claim without an
owner, we've sort of been expecting you."

"Is that so?" Thorson said dryly and laid his hand
on Dr. Drew's shoulder. "I'd like to introduce my
friend and partner, Dr. Huntley Drew. He was on
the stagecoach that O'Doone waylaid yesterday, and
he can back up my story. The doctor's an archeologist, but you may have heard of him. His name
wasn't entirely unknown in the California
diggings."

Drew came erect and nodded gravely to everyone,
and Fee quickly transferred his gaze from Thorson
to the older man, and even Rory O'Doone was impressed by the name that was synonymous with the
California vigilantes, gaping at Drew in vast astonishment and sucking in his breath sharply.

Fee lifted his broad shoulders and dropped them
and said, "That settles it, I guess. If two men of your
standing are sure that Rory was up to a bit of devil-
try, then I reckon he was. Lockhart, hasn't your
court a ruling in such cases?"

"Now wait a minute!" O'Doone said, his broad
face coloring. "You mean you ain't backing me,
Matt?"

Again Fee shrugged. "Backing you, Rory? The

whole camp seems to have the notion that you're closer to me than my right arm. I don't stand with road agents, *amigo*."

As closely as Thorson was watching, he could see no signal pass between these two, no flick of Fee's eyelid to give the lie to his words. Something seemed to cave inside Rory O'Doone, and all the bluster went out of him, but he mustered a shadow of defiance as he faced Lockhart and said, "Well, what are you going to do about it?"

There was a scattering of chairs to the back of the raised platform, and Lockhart slumped into one in sheer surprise and again had trouble finding words. "I heard Josh Hoskins' account of what happened," he said at last. "Josh told it that nothing was stolen and no real harm done, but that was only because Thorson was handier with a gun than either you or your partner, O'Doone. I'd say that the case only called for banishment. Be out of Thunder Gulch by sundown, and see that you don't show back."

Matthew Fee dug under his coat, the movement giving a glimpse of a fancy-handled forty-five belted tight against his hip. "You've done a turn or two for me, Rory," he said with a smile. "Here . . ." A buckskin poke arced through the air and O'Doone caught it sluggishly. "You might need that on the trail," Fee added.

O'Doone looked from the poke to the man who'd given it to him, as though he were trying to read some deep and tacit meaning behind this lavish gift, and he began to say something, then changed his mind. He made his way down the aisle and to the door and was gone, and Thorson let himself down to the bench, between Ginny and Dr. Drew, and found that he was weak with the aftermath of the tension that had held him so long. In the heavy silence that followed O'Doone's departure, a dozen men likewise sank to their seats, and the hush was heavy and oppressive until Fee broke it by saying, "You were having an election, weren't you? Lockhart, you'd better get on with your business."

"We started out with one nominee," said Lockhart. "Now we haven't even got him."

When Matthew Fee smiled it drew little crow's-feet at the corners of his eyes. "No candidate? Who's better qualified than young Mr. Thorson, son of our first and best marshal. If he's heir to the discovery claim, he's certainly one of us and eligible. If it's a nomination you want, I nominate him!"

That was the way it happened, and it came so quickly that it gave Thorson no time to seek out the motive behind Matthew Fee's act. Yet because he was certain that Fee's game was only for the good of Fee, and because he knew by some nameless instinct that he'd dealt the man a bad blow today and earned his enmity in spite of Fee's repudiation of Rory O'Doone, Thorson's first impulse was to refuse the nomination. Yet he still carried a clear picture of Jamieson Hazzard sprawled in the dust of the street, and he remembered the grief of Belle Kincaid and Virginia Drew, and, in answer to Lockhart's questioning glance, he said clearly, "I accept, sir."

Lockhart ran his eyes across the murmuring crowd. "Any other nominations?" he asked and waited while a minute ran its slow course, and all that while Matthew Fee stood in the center of the aisle, his thumbs hooked in the armholes of his waistcoat, and smiled benignly.

Then: "Them's that voting for Mister Thorson say 'aye,'" Lockhart ordered and had the last of his words drowned out by the thunderous response that came from the assemblage. And in this manner Tod Thorson was unanimously elected marshal of Thunder Gulch, and he found a certain irony in the reflection that he was probably the first candidate to win the vote of both the honest element and the men of the opposition.

Matthew Fee came down the aisle toward him while the building still echoed to that single voice of acclamation, and Fee extended his hand and said, "I'll be the first to congratulate you, Thorson. If you're half the marshal your father was, you'll find no complaints from any of us. And your duties will be light, I reckon. Thunder Gulch hasn't even got a jail."

It was Tod Thorson's queer thought that he'd won the first victory today, but that Matthew Fee, in nominating him, had won the second, and he wondered what strange and sinister reasoning had prompted the man to force him into office. But all he said was, "No jail? Then we'll build one." And he found a way to overlook Fee's extended hand.

Matthew Fee laughed, a ponderous, booming laugh that rolled up from the great depth of him. "Build a jail? A good idea," he said. "Why don't you drop in sometime, and we'll talk it over. I have an office over my Hurdy-Gurdy House, and you can usually find me there. We'll have a lot to discuss, you and I. You must come and see me."

"I will," Thorson said. "Sooner than you think."

They were to bury Jamieson Hazzard that evening; it didn't do to keep a body too long at this season of the year. The funeral was scheduled for sundown, and at that hour when the dusk came to mellow the diggings, brushing away its more ghastly scars, Tod Thorson and Dr. Drew joined Ginny at her cabin. The girl had donned a darker dress and sat waiting in the shadows, her hands held listlessly in her lap, her face a solemn blur, so pale and strained that Thorson wondered how much of her had died today.

He fingered the badge that Zeke Lockhart had

given him this afternoon, and he said, "I'm wondering about your plans. Dr. Drew and I are moving into my father's house. You see, we're partners in the mining property Lars Thorson left here, and the doctor has already moved his luggage from the Empire House. There is plenty of room for you, too, in the stone house. Won't you come with us?"

"No," Ginny said. "I'll be renting out this cabin; there are newcomers who'll be glad to get it. But I'm moving into Pi's old quarters in the *Trumpet* building. I've had time for thinking, and there isn't much choice for me. What he started, I'll have to finish. Someone must run the *Trumpet*."

"And you'll do it alone?"

"Pi taught me the game, all of it. I wonder if he guessed there'd be a day when I'd need to know."

Thorson gave Dr. Drew a glance, but the older man only shrugged and said, "She knows what she wants, and she's a woman now. It isn't for me to choose her pathway."

"It may be a good idea, in any case," Thorson decided. "The diggings needs a paper and there's no one else to give them one. I've put my finger on the thing that's wrong here, and Lockhart told me I was right when we had a talk after the election. There's no organization among the honest miners. That was obvious at miners' court when Rory O'Doone, a proved road agent, was backed by friends who would have defied Lockhart. The first job is to wake up the miners to the need for uniting. The second is to organize them. Will you use the *Trumpet* to help me do those things, Ginny?"

"It was Pi's own plan," she said. "Yes, I'll help you all I can."

"I'm wondering," Dr. Drew said with a frown, "just what Matthew Fee hoped to accomplish when he had you made marshal."

"Whatever it was," Thorson said darkly, "he's going to be disappointed."

"I hope so," Drew commented. He stepped to the doorway of the cabin and glanced to where the sunset was making the mountains into a glory of fire and gold. "Hadn't we better be on our way?" he said.

They came out of the cabin then, and Ginny took them in the direction of a distant plot of ground on a flat beyond the last of the shacks, and they walked in silence, the three of them, until they saw the picket fence that enclosed the gulch's cemetery, and Ginny stiffened at Thorson's side. "We came this way often," she said. "Sometimes, when an edition was ready for the press, we'd stroll here to get a breath of air to clear our heads—" She set her teeth against her lip and said no more, but Thorson knew who'd walked this way with her, and he put his hand on her arm to steady her.

There was quite a scatteration of graves beyond that picket fence, for Thunder Gulch's cemetery had grown with the same swiftness as the boom-camp. They came threading among the graves, finding some marked with wooden headboards, already faded, and some with granite boulders, hauled down from the hills to make rugged, silent sentinels atop a resting place. One such was the grave of Lars Thorson, and Tod tarried there briefly, seeing the brave display of wild flowers that broke the bleakness of the drab mound, and guessing whose hands had put them there.

Yonder, where a swelling group of people gathered, was a newly dug grave, the heaped dirt glistening dully in the last of the light, and beside it lay the rough pine box that held the remains of Jamieson Hazzard. These things Dr. Drew had arranged, and a man in ministerial black stood waiting, book in hand, and the assemblage had bared its heads.

There were many men here, and women too, and one of them was Belle Kincaid. She'd dug into her luggage for a dress that made her like something carved from ebony. Thorson spoke her name beneath his breath, and Ginny went to the woman at once, and there were no words between the two of them as they stood together.

Gray-headed Zeke Lockhart disengaged himself from a group of men and came to Thorson and Dr. Drew and shook hands with each and said, "The service is about ready to start. We've been waiting for you."

Thorson saw the Chinaman then, standing off apart from the others, a tall, round-shouldered figure wearing a padded jacket of Chinese silk rather than the shapeless black alpaca that was usually the garb of his people. There'd been Chinese at the meeting hall this afternoon, but somehow Thorson hadn't expected to find one here, and his surprised look wrung an explanation from Lockhart.

"Quong Lee," Lockhart said. "He's head man of the Chinks in these diggings, and a white man if there ever was one. He and Hazzard were very good friends. Knew each other back in the California diggings, I believe. Quong's an amazing galoot. He's half-blind, speaks our language better than most of us, and has a store of book learning. I'll introduce you, if you'd like."

"Do that," Thorson said.

Dr. Drew had wandered off, and Lockhart led Thorson to the Chinese and said the proper words, and Quong Lee bowed gravely and said, "Is good. Such a great honor leaves me tongueless . . ."

The parson began thumbing the pages of his book, his voice rising shrill yet solemn, loud enough to reach to the far fringe of the crowd. Thorson bowed his head with the others and listened to the long prayer and the longer eulogy that followed, and wondered at the worth of words at a time like this. And at long last the parson intoned, "Ashes to ashes . . . dust to dust . . ." And the men who were to take this as their cue began to lower the pine box, and there was the restless stirring among the crowd that comes when tension is suddenly released.

Thorson glanced at the two women who had loved Jamieson Hazzard, each in a different way, and found it significant that Ginny Drew, who'd gone to comfort the older woman, was weeping silently, yet Belle Kincaid remained dry-eyed, her face like something carved from the stone of the hills, her eyes burning with a strange and terrible intensity. He wondered if the next stage would take her out of Thunder Gulch, and somehow knew that it wouldn't.

Lockhart said, "A nice turnout. Hazzard would have liked this. Every man here was his friend."

There were quite a lot of them. Thorson had wondered if Matthew Fee would dare show himself at the funeral, but the man was nowhere to be seen. There were many faces that Thorson remembered from the meeting hall, but none were the men who'd backed Rory O'Doone. And thus it came to him that one force, and one only, was represented at this gathering, and he ran his glance over the group and measured its collective strength and found it mighty. His eyes sought out Dr. Drew, who was making a great business of blowing his nose, and he recalled that man's work in California. And Thorson's thought was that here was fresh material for the proper shaping.

The shoveled clods thudded monotonously onto the top of the lowered pine box. There was nothing more to be done for Jamieson Hazzard now. Only Hazzard's dream remained. All the rest had become ashes to ashes . . . dust to dust . . .

Chapter Five
FACED CARDS

At that dark hour when Thunder Gulch was fully awakening to its boisterous and noisome night life, Tod Thorson threaded his way toward the flamboyant front of the Hurdy-Gurdy House, mindful of his intention to have a talk with Matthew Fee as soon as possible. The street was an endless stream of milling pleasure-seekers now, and the dusty road between the facing buildings was thronged with rumbling wagons, and all the hurly-burly of a raw and growing town was here.

One wagon held Thorson's eye, a high-sided freighter, for the drummer, Ed Folinsbee, sat perched beside the swearing driver, clutching his luggage and his derby as though they held his chances at eternity. Folinsbee was keeping his word and leaving Thunder Gulch by the quickest means, his terror and his need for haste so great that he wasn't even waiting for the comparative comfort of the weekly stagecoach. And Thorson put a somber and thoughtful speculation upon the man's departure and saw it as a symbol boding no good for the camp. Then he shrugged and elbowed on to Fee's place.

Shoving in through the door, Thorson paused just beyond the threshold, finding an establishment that differed from anything he'd ever seen in a varied lifetime. Saloons he had known, and dancehalls too, but this combination, along with its obvious sidelines, made a merger of all the ways of wickedness to be found on the frontier. Life had a fast pulse here; he could feel the throb of it above the steady beat of the music.

Most of the ground floor was given over to a single large room with a bar at its far end and a railing to separate the place of drinking from the place of dancing. Beyond the railing stood a huddle of men, thick-muscled from working their sluices, and dressed in their colorful best. On this side of the barrier were the hurdy-gurdies, the dancing women, a collection of femininity from the four corners of the land, overly painted and garishly dressed. Looking at them, Thorson wondered how many had traded the last of their dreams for the tinsel of this place.

To the right of the room was a raised platform with a four-piece orchestra which had just struck up a waltz. "Take your partners for the next dance," a heavy-voiced houseman was calling, and the miners surged forward to pay a dollar in gold dust for a ticket worth a few brief minutes on the floor.

Thorson spied Fee then; the man was standing at the far end of the bar. Finding his way among the dancers and being cursed soundly by many a clumsy-footed miner thrown out of step by an effort to avoid a collision, Thorson made his way to the railing, hauled himself over it and came upon Fee. The big man smiled broadly and said, "Evening, Marshal. A drink?"

Thorson shook his head. "We were to have a talk," he reminded the man.

"Sure," said Fee. "My office is upstairs."

He led the way, skirting past a gambling wing where chips clinked to the touch of nervous fingers and the low whine of roulette wheels was lost beneath the blaring music, and Thorson followed after him, climbing a carpeted stair and coming down a dimly lighted second-story hallway to a room at the front of the building.

Fee's office was big and ornate, a massive desk centering it, and the rug that covered the floor had

come all the way from the Levant. The chairs were
many and plush-covered, the costly sideboard was
scrolled and veneered, and a banjo clock on the wall
loudly ticked off the marching minutes. Upon all
this lavishness Thorson placed a quick estimation
and whistled softly. "You like things comfortable, I
see," he said.

Fee crossed to the sideboard. He wore a ruffled
shirtfront tonight, and a diamond solitaire winked
back from the mirror, and his hands did quick
things with an array of glassware. "Here is whiskey
you can't buy over my bar," he said. "What is your
choice?"

"Nothing tonight, thanks."

Fee arched his eyebrows. With the lamplight to
soften the lines of his face, he looked devilishly
young. "Will you try a cigar, then?" he asked. "I
have them brought up from Salt Lake weekly."

"There's nothing like a good cigar," said Thorson
and reached for one, and Fee was quick to supply
the match.

"Have a chair," he suggested.

"Sure," said Thorson and dropped into one. Fee
placed himself behind his desk and laced his fingers
across his shirtfront. "What's on your mind, Marshal?" he asked amiably. "Not that new jail?"

"No, nothing special," said Thorson. "I've built a
theory or two today, Fee. Maybe you can tell me
how right or wrong they are. First, there was Rory
O'Doone. As I see it, Rory's predicament put you in
a tight. Half the crowd was ready to go at the throat
of the other half, but one bunch of boys needed your
cue. Rory had already convicted himself. If you'd
backed him at that moment, there'd have been a
showdown and the whole camp would have known
just how you stood. So you tossed Rory to the
wolves. Or pretended to. You've got a head for quick
thinking, Fee."

Fee laughed his booming laugh. "It comes in handy," he agreed. "You can see for yourself, Thorson, that I'm not half the ogre some folks make me out to be. I run this place, yes. It attracts the kind of men who are probably behind most of the sluggings and robberies and high-grading that goes on in the diggings. But that doesn't prove I'm kingpin of the road agents. Rory O'Doone worked for me at times, that's true. But whatever took him to the top of the Wolverine was his own idea. So why should I have backed him up today?"

"You tell me," Thorson countered dryly.

"I want the confidence of the people of the gulch," Fee continued. "I can turn it into gold. Look at it this way: I'm one of the most influential citizens. I have my own claim at the diggings and a stamp mill I've freighted in. I run the Hurdy-Gurdy, and I run a freight line to Shoshone once a week. But do most of the miners use my stamp mill? No, they pile up their ore against the day when they'll get the guts to risk taking it out. And they won't hire my wagons to tote it for them. That's because they believe I'm the man behind gents like Rory O'Doone. They don't trust me any farther than they could tote a ton of ore on their backs."

"I had a talk with Zeke Lockhart after the election," Thorson said. "He tells it that your price for the use of your stamp mill or the use of your wagons is so high that the miners might better leave their gold in the ground than pay it. Could it be that the road agent scare is to force the miners to use your equipment whether they want to or not?"

He thought that blunt thrust might be the spark to set off Fee's wrath, and he waited for the explosion, but the big man only shook his head. "You can see the opinion they have," he said and winked ponderously. "That's what I'm trying to break down."

Thorson dropped his cigar into a cuspidor. "And

is that why you backed me for marshal? I've had some ideas about that, but none of them make sense."

Fee shrugged. "I backed you because I wanted a man of your caliber in that office. You're Lars Thorson's son, and even if you don't stack up to him in size, I'm taking it for granted that you're of the same fighting breed. I knew Lars well. He's the only man who ever whipped me in a hand-to-hand fight. I'd rather have a Thorson on my side. But you might say Lars was a little old-fashioned. I'm thinking you and I will get along better."

"Meaning?"

"There's a good living to be made in Thunder Gulch while the camp lasts. But I'm not out to hog all the gold. Those who string along with me will get their share. Live and let live, that's my rule. We could do business, Marshal."

"I'm to be blind to the things I shouldn't see?" Thorson asked. "Deaf to the things I shouldn't hear?"

Fee chose his words carefully. "That's one way of putting it. What's your stand, Thorson?"

In the moment of silence that followed, the thin wail of a fiddle seeped up from the room below, making a melancholy and incongruous note in this lavish room. Thorson came up from his chair and crossed to a window and looked down upon the street below. The night had claimed it, but the light from many windows splashed broadly across the dusty way, laying a saffron pattern. Thorson raised his right hand and looked along the pointed index finger, and his eye ran to the spot where Jamieson Hazzard had fallen.

"One of the reasons why the people of this camp have their own ideas about your being a good citizen is because the *Trumpet* opened their eyes," Thorson guessed. "I talked to the undertaker today.

He said the bullet drove downward at an angle. You killed him, didn't you, Fee?"

"A shot from my window?" Fee scoffed. "I wondered who'd be the first to think of that. But Hazzard might have turned around as he fell, and the shot could have come from any second-story window along the street. Yes, Hazzard was a thorn in my side. But he didn't sting that much."

"You killed him, or you had it done," Thorson insisted. "And that's one big reason why the answer is no. The J in my name stands for Jamieson. I was named after him, Fee. There were three men in the California diggings who were inseparable friends. Lars Thorson was one, a big Norwegian giant with an itching foot. The other two were Jamieson Hazzard who planned a great book that he never got around to writing, and Huntley Drew, a scientist with a passion for justice. It's queer that their trails went separate ways only to cross again in Thunder Gulch. Lars brought Hazzard here, I know. And Lars and Hazzard had a dream—a dream of a town that would still stand, long after the gold bubble broke. You killed Hazzard, and you're trying to kill that dream. And that makes two reasons why we're against each other from here on out."

All the good humor went out of Fee's face, and all the pretense was gone too, and he said, "You're a fool, Thorson! Yes, I've heard Lars Thorson talk of the town he was going to build. He hoped there'd be a railroad coming over the Wolverines, and he had a pretty picture of Thunder Gulch blossoming out with paved streets and all the trimmings. Bah! I've seen these boom-camps before! They're worth only what can be wrung out of them while they last!"

He came to his feet, spreading his hands in a gesture that encompassed all this room. "Here's as much civilization as this half-acre of hell will ever see," he declared. "Or should I build a stone house to match Lars Thorson's? I'm bringing in a planing mill of my own, friend. I'm lining all the Hurdy-Gurdy House with boards, and my freighters will shortly deliver a load of wallpaper. I understand it will have a design of blue birds, the symbol of happiness. Will I meet your qualifications as a citizen and town-builder then, Thorson?''

"You're making fun of an idea that's so big it's beyond your understanding!" Thorson said hotly. "But at the same time, you know that as long as there are places like this one, the people who might make a town out of these diggings will leave as quickly as their claims are worked out. And that's just why I've got to drive you out of here!"

"I see. 'The desert shall rejoice and blossom as the rose. And the parched ground shall become a pool, and the thirsty land springs of water . . .' That's from Isaiah, Thorson, and it speaks Lars Thorson's idea better than he did. You're surprised that I quote Bible, eh? For sixteen years of my life I was bound out to a Pennsylvania farmer who worked me like hell all the daylight hours and crammed Scripture into me half the night. He was a cold, flinty man who thought smiling was a sin and that a hearty laugh was proof that a man had sold himself to Satan. And since the day I broke his skull and ran away, I've had one idea I've never forgotten. The world belongs to the man who's big enough to hold it in his two hands and wring what he wants from it. It's taken a lot of living to make up for those sixteen years. And I'm just starting!"

Thorson shrugged. "You've made your choice," he said. "I've made mine."

"And I'll be living on the top of the heap when you and all your lofty-minded breed are sitting in the ashes of your high-falutin' dreams!" Fee snapped.

Thorson stepped toward the door. "We've faced

our cards, and we know how we stand. That's as it should be. And I'm driving you out, just as I promised. And I want you to know that Jamieson Hazzard isn't half as dead as you think. You wasted a bullet, Fee. There'll be a *Trumpet* issued next week, and the week after, and as long as the paper's needed. Its policy will be the same as it was before."

That hit Fee—hard. "The girl!" he said in sudden understanding. "She's going to run the paper."

"Exactly," said Thorson, but he saw the light that came swiftly to Fee's eyes and was gone again, and he wished he'd held his tongue, for now Fee had been forewarned.

Yet what had been said couldn't be unsaid, and he opened the door and stepped into the hallway and found the stairs, and he could still feel the eyes of Matthew Fee upon his back long after they'd parted company. A quadrille was coming to an end as he reached the dance floor, and the houseman cried, "Gents to the right; promenade to the bar." Thorson took advantage of the dispersing movement to make his quick way toward the door.

But before he reached it, he saw Belle Kincaid standing just this side of the threshold, and since she still wore the black gown she'd donned for Hazzard's funeral, she made a queer figure in this assemblage of tinsel and color. She stood watching, no hesitancy about her, yet Thorson was prompted to ask, "Are you looking for someone? Maybe I can help you."

She turned to regard him, and she was as wooden-faced as she'd been when he'd found her in her hotel room this morning when he'd come bringing the news of Hazzard's death. She said, "Matthew Fee. I'm told he does the hiring here."

That left Thorson speechless, but at last he blurted, "You don't mean that you intend to work in this—this place?"

She nodded.

Again he fumbled for words, wondering why he should be so careful of the pride which she had apparently abandoned, and he said, "If it's money you're needing, I would be glad to make you a loan. Please don't misunderstand me. Jamieson Hazzard was my father's friend, and therefore my friend. And there are many others here in the gulch who'd be glad of the opportunity to help you."

"It's not a matter of money," she said. "Will you tell me where I'll find Matthew Fee?"

He made one more attempt to pierce her inscrutability, to bare the motive that brought her here. "He's in his office at the end of the upper-story hallway," he said. "You'll find the stairs. But I'm wondering if you know that he is probably the man who killed Hazzard. Or at least he ordered the killing done."

"Yes, I know," she said. "I've heard the talk of this town today. Thank you." And she nodded her head and was gone with a swish of her long skirts, and he watched until the crowd enveloped her and she was lost from sight.

He went outside and into the stream of humanity pouring along the strewn planks, blending with that colorful current. He whistled softly and asked himself questions, but there were no answers for them. Then he saw a light in the window of the *Thunder Gulch Trumpet* across the way, and he dismissed Belle Kincaid from his mind.

Crossing the street obliquely, he headed for the newspaper building, his stride long and steady.

Chapter Six
SILENTLY IN THE SHADOWS

For a long time now Ginny Drew had sat before the battered desk in the *Trumpet* office, the shaded lamp enclosing her in a cone of light that made a shimmering halo of her honey-colored hair. She had come here directly after Jamieson Hazzard's funeral, motivated by some compelling need to write his obituary while her grief was at its strongest. She had sat through timeless hours while the night claimed Thunder Gulch and the street became thronged, but she was oblivious to the restless parade passing the doorway. Her pencil was held tightly in her hand; the paper was blank before her.

She did not know it, but she was tired, tireder than she'd ever been. Grief is a relentless taskmaster, and the other excitements of the day had also harried her. A physician might have spoken of shock or emotional reaction. Ginny only knew that she still had the queer sensation of being detached from herself, and that the Ginny Drew who'd lost one father and found another today was therefore a stranger whom she could view with a curious unconcern.

Not that she was devoting much thought to herself. It was easier to let her mind drift aimlessly, to touch upon one thing and another like a leaf borne lazily by an erratic river. There was Belle Kincaid, for instance. It took a woman's heart to sense the whole tragedy of the untimely coming of the other woman. Ginny had glimpsed what lay behind Belle's eyes—and understood. After the funeral she'd asked the older woman to come and share her quarters. But Jamieson Hazzard's fiancée had only shaken her head and gone her wordless way.

And there was Dr. Huntley Drew, who was a name on the back of a book, and who was also her father. She had built a thousand mental pictures of him in the past, painting each to suit a girlish fancy. He had differed from all of them, and as yet she'd failed to grasp the reality that was him. Through this long day she'd seen him often, but still they were strangers. He'd suggested remedying that this very night, if she felt up to the attempt. She appreciated his thoughtfulness in leaving her grief to run its course, and she wondered if he were waiting in that lonely stone house Lars Thorson had built. And she wished she could muster the spirit to go to him.

And Tod Thorson. He had walked into her life today too, and his name had been like a promise. What one Thorson had started, another might finish. He had looked like Lars Thorson not at all, yet at the miner's court election he had dealt the might of Matthew Fee a hurt that would be a long time healing. He— But Tod Thorson was standing in the doorway, regarding her with a smiling solemnity and saying, "Hello."

"Oh, hello," she said. "You startled me. I've been daydreaming."

"And I've been looking into the welfare of our growing city," he said. "Ginny, will you do a favor for me?"

She found time now to notice that he had the knack of being charming without overworking at it, and she wondered how many people had ever refused him when he'd asked a favor. But she said, incongruously, "Where did you keep yourself all the years that Lars Thorson was tramping the West?"

"Here and there," he said. He came inside and laid his beaver on the desk, and the lamplight put a dark sheen upon his hair. "When mother died, Lars put me in a home in St. Louis. He managed to get back and see me on the average of once every five years, but he kept the money coming in between times. Come to think of it, you must have known him better than I! But I heard about him wherever I went, and I did a lot of traveling after I grew up. I was representative for a St. Louis trading company that had a couple of packets on the Missouri and some interests in gold and furs. I'm no tenderfoot."

"No, I think not," she said. "What is this favor you want?"

"Will you move to the stone house to live, at least for a while?" he asked. "I'll bunk here, in Hazzard's quarters. I'd rather it was that way."

"Why?" she asked bluntly.

He hesitated, but only for a moment. "I just finished talking to Matthew Fee," he said. "We sort of declared war all around. But I made one mistake. I just the same as told him that the *Trumpet* would be siding me against him. He won't be forgetting that."

She said, "I promised Doct—father—that I'd come up and spend the evening with him, if I felt that I could. We have so much to talk about. I'll go now and see him. And I'll tell him that I'm taking over your room for the time being."

"You're a good girl," he said. "I was afraid you might have some fool notion about deserting a post."

She looked at him sharply, and if there'd been so much as a hint of laughter in his eyes, she'd have raised enough spirit to rebel against his idea. As it was, his face was grave, and she said, "There's a place for heroics, and a place for common sense. That's one of the things I learned from Pi. If Matthew Fee should strike at us by night, it will be better if there's a man and a gun to greet him."

He placed her cloak about her shoulders and leaned and blew out the lamp, and she saw his face, a pale blur above her, as he said, "Good night." Then she slipped through the doorway and into the street.

Her route took her along the gulch to the point where the buildings thinned, and then she turned to her right and began climbing the wandering pathway that led to the miners' court building. But where the pathway forked, she went to the left, heading for the great stone house that stood upon a shoulder of the slope. No lights burned in any of the windows facing her way, she noticed, and she wondered if Dr. Drew had already retired, then decided it was more likely that he'd gone to have a look at the camp at this roistering hour.

Lars Thorson had been a big man, and he'd needed a lot of house. He'd built unstintingly and to no fixed design, the structure of his creation sprawling haphazardly on the hillside. There was a porch and a ponderous door at one end of it, and Ginny reached the shadows before the door, her knuckles poised, but she did not knock. How could so feeble a sound carry into the depth of this great pile? She put her hand to the door and was surprised when it gave beneath her touch.

That wasn't as it should be. She remembered the many years her father had followed lonely trails in the depth of the Yucatán jungles, and she forgave him this oversight, reasoning that a man whose castle has been a canvas tent would hardly be overly alert to a need for locks. She made a mental note to speak to him on the subject, but she was glad that she wouldn't have to spend lengthy, laborious minutes beating upon the door. Then she pushed into a hallway that was a straight tunnel of darkness.

But no, there were doors leading off this hallway, and one was open, and the tag-ends of lamplight spilled from it into the hall. She hastily drew upon her memory of this house, and it was her recollec-

tion that that particular room was a sort of storeroom, scantily furnished and hardly the place where
a man would be spending an evening. And because
she was suddenly cold with the certainty that it
wasn't her father who was in that room, the last of
her lethargy fell from her, and she was vitally alive
to a need for caution.

She came down that hallway with no more sound
than the passing of a shadow, sliding one foot ahead
of the other and taking a great deal of time at it. She
made it to the doorway and peered inside and saw
who was in there and what he was up to, and she
strangled an impulse to scream.

The luggage of Dr. Drew, lately removed from the
Empire House, had been placed in this room. There
were two telescope grips and a huge, leather-bound
trunk, and there was no mistaking them for they
bore the initials H. D. Tod Thorson's luggage was
here too, piled in a farther corner, but it held no
interest for the man who'd come out of the night.
He was crouched on the floor, the bulk of him like
some great bloated spider against the feeble light
from a shaded lamp upon a small table. He had
opened both grips and the trunk, and a scattering of
clothes, personal belongings, books and letters
made a mottled pattern upon the floor.

The man had a leather-bound book in his hand
and was avidly thumbing its pages, scanning one
after another of them. Ginny guessed that the book
was a diary or journal of sorts. He held the book
closer to the lamp, and in this manner his broad
face fell into the light, and the tiny, crescent-shaped
scar at the tip of his left cheekbone was highlighted.
Ginny drew in her breath sharply. For here was
Rory O'Doone, banished today by the miners' court
and supposedly hours gone from these diggings!

And she knew that he'd heard that slight betraying sound she'd made. He turned his ponderous

head, his eyes questing the shadows. He came
slowly to his feet and moved toward the doorway,
and there was no strength in her to turn and flee.
For a moment they stood facing each other, and he
might easily have felled her with his fist and gone
his way. But astonishment had laid a heavy hand
upon him, and he was all instinct at the moment—
and his instinct was to flee.

Turning, he lunged across the storeroom, jerking
at the drawn shade of its only window, and he had it
up and was hoisting the sash and laying one leg
across the sill when Ginny came after him. She was
never to give herself credit for courage when she
looked back upon this hour. She only knew that he
still held that diary in his hand, and it seemed the
most important thing in the world to keep him from
taking it along.

She came like an aroused cat, all claws and fury.
She pounced upon him, striking blindly, and he
said, "Damn!" with pain and anger in his voice and
gave her a violent shove. Her cloak fell to the floor
and one of her shoulders was bared where his hand
had struck her, but she came back at him again,
seizing his hand and sinking her teeth into it. He
dropped the diary, but his free fist balled and she
felt the weight of it against her cheek, a grazing
blow.

It was enough to send her to her knees, and he
pulled himself free and went out of the window, and
she tried to steady herself in a spinning world as she
heard his boots slogging in frantic retreat. She let
herself slump to the floor and she lay there clutching her father's diary and fighting against an over-
whelming nausea and finding the strength to conquer it. When she came to her feet, grasping the
little table to steady herself, she reeled out of the
room and down the hallway, and in her haste she

left the great door open behind her as she stumbled across the porch and down the trail.

She was running frantically by the time she reached the bottom of the gulch, her hair, loosened in the struggle, bannering out behind her. But the breeze of her own making was like a cool, steadying hand, and under its ministration her head cleared and her terror ebbed. She was surprised to find the diary still clutched in her hand. Thrusting it into the front of her dress, she stumbled onward . . .

For the first few minutes after Ginny had left the *Trumpet* office, Tod Thorson had stood in the darkness watching her through the window until she was caught by the crowd and carried from his sight. Then he began a systematic examination of the premises, feeling his way along silently and finding his eyes growing more accustomed to the darkness.

The office held little to interest him, so he groped out into the press room behind. The press, the tables and the cases of type loomed grotesquely, and he might have had trouble making his way, but there was a window to the rear of the building and it gave a little light. He gravitated toward that window and found that it opened by sliding to one side and that it was held shut by a crude catch that would offer no great resistance to a determined intruder. He put his mind to seeking a ready way to remedy this, and could find none.

Feeling his way along the wall from the window, he found the rear door. It was heavy enough, and barred from the inside. This fact carefully noted, he came back to the office and put his hand to the other door leading off from this front room. It gave into Jamieson Hazzard's quarters, a bedroom and a kitchen of sorts.

There was no rear door in this part of the build-

ing, but there were two windows, both of them
small.

His investigation completed, Thorson stretched
himself, fully clothed, upon Hazzard's bed. He felt
no desire for sleep; the doings of the day had sharp-
ened his nerves to a high point. He lay there in the
darkness, listening to the sounds of Thunder Gulch
all around him, for the chinking had fallen out between some of the logs of this structure, and he
made a great game of sorting these sounds, one
from another, and identifying them. There was Matthew Fee's stamp mill, ceaseless and thunderous.
There was the distant music of the Hurdy-Gurdy
House, and the eternal beat—beat—beat of dancing
feet. And the strewn planks that served in place of
sidewalks also served as sounding boards for the
feet that trod upon them.

One man was lurching along unsteadily, and
Thorson smiled and wondered how much whiskey
was beneath that fellow's belt. Another came upon
soft soles, his step mincing but hardly feminine, and
Thorson had a hard time identifying him until he
remembered the Chinese who also dwelt in these
diggings. That took his mind to Quong Lee, head
man of the Orientals, whom he'd met, briefly, at
Hazzard's funeral. He reminded himself that he'd
see Quong Lee another night, and to greater purpose, for the Chinese of Thunder Gulch fitted into a
plan half-formed in his mind.

Then he became conscious of the footsteps in the
alley behind the *Trumpet* building.

They sounded an instant warning note, for they
were furtive beyond any honest need, the cautious
movements of three or four men stalking silently in
the shadows. He waited then, content to see what
move was to be made before he formulated one to
counter it. He could hear nothing for a lengthy minute, and he'd almost concluded that he'd been mis-

taken and that whoever had walked the alley had gone on to its farther end. But no, there was a faint scraping sound from the region of the press room, a rasping click, and a window made a slight squeal as it was slid aside.

So soon, Thorson thought, and was glad that he'd made his arrangement with Ginny at once, instead of waiting until another night. Then he came to his feet. He'd left two doors open, the one leading from Hazzard's quarters into the office, and the one giving off the office into the press room. He eased through both of these doorways, moving carefully and cautiously, and, once into the press room, he saw that the dim square of the window was blotted out by a looming form.

He let the man climb through the window. He heard the fellow groping about, heard him curse softly as he collided with something in the darkness. Then the fellow found the door and swung back the bar, and the door bulged inward and other men came easing into the room. Three or four of them. Thorson couldn't be sure. But he knew they were spreading out, groping their way through the room, but he had his gun in his hand now, and he said distinctly, "Something I can do for you boys?"

A man wheezed in surprise, another cursed angrily. But one among them had a presence of mind that proved Thorson's undoing. He was standing at the end of a littered table, was Thorson, and he had no knowledge of the nearness of this one marauder until the fellow shoved the table against him, a hard, quick movement that numbed Thorson's hip.

Hurled off balance, Thorson went down, and the instant that he did, they came swarming upon him. He tried to bring his gun into play, but a man set his boot heel against Thorson's wrist, and even though the act had been done unwittingly in the darkness, it served to send a lancing pain through Thorson's hand, and the gun fell from his fingers. He felt the press of bodies smothering him, and he put all his strength against them, coming to his knees and then to his feet, and scattering his assailants with quick movements of elbows and knees.

That gave him room for fighting, and he lashed out wildly and knew a savage satisfaction because his first blow found a man and drew a gusty sigh from him. But they were all around him, and one piled onto his back, and Thorson made a titanic effort to hurl the man over his head. This man was a big one, and the weight of him staggered Thorson, and he lurched sideways. The two of them went down, and a type case crashed over at the same time, and Thorson found himself on the floor in a scatteration of type, most of it still moist and inky.

"Jump him, you fools!" the man on the floor barked, and Thorson was almost certain it was Fee, himself.

He managed to get to his feet before his opponent did, but there were two more waiting to hurl themselves upon him. He buried his fist in the pit of one's stomach, and his second blow was aimed at a shadowy blob of face. But his arm was caught from behind, and the blow didn't go where he'd wanted it to. He spun about, jabbing his elbow into the face of the man who was clinging to him, and something grazed his right temple at that moment, and he knew that one of them had finally contrived to get at him with a gun-barrel.

It brought him to his knees and then to the floor, and he knew that his fight against unconsciousness was going to be a losing one. He lay inert, waiting for their boots to crash against his ribs, trying desperately the while to gather the ragged remnants of his strength, and he heard the voice of one of them as from a great and dark-filled distance. "Get it over

with and get out of here fast!" the speaker said.
"We've made enough noise to raise the dead!"

They were instantly busying themselves at some
bustling task, and he felt a mighty need to know
what they were doing, but the shadows were deepening for him. They were sloshing something about,
and the odor was acutely familiar, yet it seemed
hours before he recognized it as coal oil. But with
that one fact to peg his thoughts upon, he understood everything then, and he knew they were going
to fire the building.

A match flared fitfully and was lowered to the
floor, and a sheet of flame sprang up. It made a
lurid backdrop for the milling men, and they were
outlined against it for a fleeting moment, and then
they were gone, the back door banging shut after
them. He was alone in the burning building, and he
had to muster the strength to get out of it. He tried
to come to his knees, and twice he almost succeeded. But his strength wasn't great enough, and
he was sick with the assurance that it would never
be great enough and that he must lie here and let
the spreading fire inch closer to him.

That was his last thought before unconsciousness
claimed him.

Chapter Seven
THE VIKING'S WAY

Tod Thorson came back to consciousness a few moments later, drawn upward out of oblivion and a deep and tangled dream of disaster by the compelling instinct to live. He could taste the blood of his recent battle upon his lips, and he could see that rearing wall of flame, its nearness making his eyes sting and filling him with a consuming fear that might have given way to hysteria if he hadn't put his will against it. The fire had veered away from the press, he noticed; the biggest blaze was in a corner of the room. This gave his mind something to work at, and it became a grim necessity to discover what burned so briskly.

He thought of all the things this building held before it came to him that the paper stock had been piled yonderly and the fire was eating into it.

Shaking his head to rid himself of his buzzing bewilderment, he tried again to come up off the floor. He was on one knee when he felt hands grasping at his armpits. "Who—?" he said uncertainly, and a sob and a murmured word answered him. The fact that Ginny Drew was in this burning building was like a dash of icy water in his face.

She was trying to draw him toward the doorway giving into the office. She was throwing all her strength into the task, but the weight of him was no easy thing for a girl her size to handle and he could give her no help. The slowness of her progress brought him a new and greater fear that was not for himself, and he said shrilly, "You fool! You damn' little fool! Get out of here!"

She made no answer, keeping her strength for another need, and he cursed her again and again, then fell to begging her to leave him. He tried to twist free of her grip, but hadn't the strength for that. She had him to the threshold of the office now, and the outer door, facing the street, was opening, the quick draft lifting the flames higher as men came surging into the building. Thorson felt himself lifted bodily, and the coolness of the night was like a woman's soothing hand in a feverish hour. He let himself go unconscious again, and when he opened his eyes he was propped against a building across the street and Ginny was loosening his shirt.

He said, "Those others would have come too late if you hadn't gotten me as far as the door, Ginny. I—" A new and urgent thought took hold of him, and he tried to pull himself to a stand. "The *Trumpet!*" he cried. "The whole outfit will be ashes—!"

She put her hands on his shoulders, keeping him down. "Hush!" she said, and he found a wealth of comfort in her voice. "Others will save what can be saved. The fire company's here."

Until now, Thorson hadn't known that Thunder Gulch had a volunteer fire company, but when he looked across the street he saw the queue of men stretching to the doorway of the *Trumpet* building from the well that stood across from the Hurdy-Gurdy House. Buckets were passing briskly along the line, and the gathering crowd was helping by hurrying to water barrels that had been placed intermittently along the street. Soon the bell atop the miners' court building began to boom, but most of the men of the diggings were already here, needing no such tocsin. Fire was the greatest hazard that might threaten a frontier camp, and there were older men in Thunder Gulch who could remember that San Francisco, in the turbulent days of its gold rush, had burned down eight times in eighteen months. San Francisco had been rebuilt, and, so long as there was gold in the ground, Thunder Gulch would also rise out of its own ashes. But if the fire could be stopped from spreading, there were stout men to lend a hand.

It filled Tod with a stifling impotency to watch them work. This he suffered in silence as long as he could, but when Ginny left him to hurry away and help, he tried again to stand and found that time and the touch of the night had wrought something of a cure. He teetered unsteadily for a minute, bracing himself against the wall. Then he tried one step and another, and in this manner he reached the *Trumpet* building.

The bucket brigade straggled through the office and into the press room, and he squirmed along that sweating chain and into the smoking interior, finding it black and hazy and nauseating with the stench of charred, water-soaked wood and burned paper. But the flames were out, the damage not too great, and he drew some consolation from that as he came to the street again. Zeke Lockhart was here, barking orders; the man was captain of the fire company as well as head of the miners' court. Dr. Drew made a link in the bucket brigade, smoke-begrimed yet making a fine figure as he stood hatless, the wind brushing the hair back from his high brow.

There were women in the bucket brigade too, Thorson realized. Ginny was one; the others were from the Hurdy-Gurdy House. And Matthew Fee had also taken a place in the line.

That was the greatest surprise of all. The man had stripped off his coat, and the diamond solitaire on his ruffled shirtfront caught the splash of yellow light from an open doorway and spun a dazzling star from it. Zeke Lockhart brushed by, saying, "You can disband, men. Fire's out." The queue broke around Thorson, and Dr. Drew came to one side of

him and Ginny to the other as he faced Matthew
Fee.

"How are you feeling, Marshal?" Fee asked. "I
was late getting here, but the story runs that you
were inside the building when the fire started. No
harm done to you, I hope."

"Not enough to worry you out of a good night's
sleep," Thorson said dryly. "I'm a little surprised to
find you here."

Fee smiled, stepped over to where he'd dropped
his coat, shook the dust from it and shrugged into
the garment. "I'm as selfish as the next man, Marshal," he said. "The way the wind's running, there
was little chance of the flames jumping the street to
my Hurdy-Gurdy House, but you never can tell
when the wind will change." He thrust out his hand.
"Congratulations on your escape," he added.

Thorson, looking down at his own hand, found it
smeared with ink, and he remembered that fight in
the darkness and the type case that had spilled over.
There'd been a man upon his back and the two of
them had gone to the floor where the moist type lay
scattered. "I hope you have no trouble washing the
ink off your hand, Fee," he said as he turned away.
"I'll say this much for you. You're not afraid of
dirtying yourself!"

Fee's smile faded and he took a quick stride, laying his hand on Thorson's shoulder and jerking him
around. "Are you accusing me of something?" Fee
demanded.

Thorson brushed Fee's hand away with an impa-
tient gesture. "Not on the evidence I've got," he
said. "But I think we understand each other, Fee."

A hot and mighty rage was building within Matthew Fee and he said, "If you were half the size of
your father, Thorson, I wouldn't have to take your
damn' insinuations! But laying a hand on you would
be like beating a child!"

"Don't let that worry you, old son," Thorson said wearily and began worming out of the tattered remnants of his coat. "From the moment you first walked into the miners' meeting, I've had a hunch there'd be a time when we'd slug it out. Let's get it over with."

But Ginny was instantly between the two men, her eyes blazing, and she turned the force of her wrath against Fee. "Can't you see that he can hardly stand!" she cried. "Haven't you done enough damage to us for one day? If it's a fight you want, we'll tell the crowd how matters stand and see if we can find a man to oblige you!"

Fee looked over her head, meeting Thorson's eyes, and in their locking gaze a challenge was made and accepted. "See you later, Thorson," Fee said and shouldered into the milling crowd and was gone.

Thorson said, "I could use some sleep."

Ginny took his arm and started up the street with him, and Dr. Drew disappeared into the crowd and came panting after them a few moments later. "I talked to Zeke Lockhart," he said. "He'll see that the *Trumpet* building is watched for the rest of the night. There's room for all of us in the stone house."

Thorson glanced at Ginny. "I haven't had time to ask you before, Ginny, but I'm wondering what brought you back to the *Trumpet* just when I needed you most."

"Rory O'Doone," she said.

"O'Doone! He's still here, in Thunder Gulch?"

She told them her story, describing her trip to the stone house and the man she'd found there and the struggle they'd had. "Father was gone," she concluded. "When I came running out of the house, I headed straight for the *Trumpet* to tell you what had happened, Tod. I found the press room in flames and you on the floor."

Reaching into her dress, she produced the book she'd snatched from O'Doone and passed it over to Dr. Drew. "I got this away from Rory," she said.

Drew's brow pleated with a frown as he thumbed the pages of the book and dropped it into a pocket. "What could O'Doone have wanted with this?" he wondered. "It's a diary of sorts—a journal I kept on our last expedition into Yucatán. It has a value—yes. But only to me. From these notes, I plan to do a book about our trip, if I can. Dr. Wish was the literary light of our combination, and I shall miss him much."

"Your partner's gone back to Mexico?" Thorson asked.

"Ab Wish is dead," Drew said gravely. "He took fever while we were in the jungles and lived only long enough to reach San Francisco. We walked a long trail together, but it came to an end."

"I'm sorry," Thorson said.

"And I. In a year's time I've lost three good friends—Ab and Lars Thorson, and now Jamieson Hazzard. It makes a man wonder where his own trail has its last turning."

Ginny's shudder transmitted itself to Thorson and he said gently, "We're all tired and overwrought. It'll be a brighter-looking world tomorrow."

They'd come toward the stone house as they talked, and as they paused on the porch, Thorson felt for his gun, then remembered that it had been left on the press room floor. But Dr. Drew dug a weapon out from under his coattails and kept it in his hand as they opened the door and stepped into the hallway.

That long tunnel was indeed dark now, and they felt along to the storeroom where Ginny had found Rory O'Doone. The window was still up, the shade flapping in a breeze that had blown out the lamp. Thorson closed the window while Dr. Drew got the

lamp aglow again, the blossoming light showing
them the havoc O'Doone had wrought, the opened
grips and trunk and the scattered letters and books
and personal belongings.

Drew knelt and scooped up these things, deposit-
ing them in the trunk and tossing the diary in after
them. He said, "I waited for you tonight, Ginny.
When you didn't come, I went out to the diggings
for a breath of fresh air and was looking at the discovery claim when word came of a fire in camp. I
can't tell you how sorry I am that I wasn't here
when you walked into trouble."

"It's over now," she said. "But we can never
leave a door unlocked in Thunder Gulch again."

Thorson nodded, lifting the lamp from the table.
With their shadows pacing them, they went upstairs
to the second floor, Dr. Drew turning into the room
he'd taken over that afternoon, while Thorson led
Ginny to the one he'd intended occupying.

"I'll find another," he said as he placed the lamp
on a mantel. Regarding her, he saw how weary she
was, yet he found something compelling in the picture she made, her honey-colored hair straggling
about her face, her hazel eyes shadowy. He placed
his hands on her shoulders and said gently, "How
can I thank you for what you did tonight?"

Then he kissed her. He had meant to kiss her as a
friend kisses a friend, but when his lips touched
hers he knew it was not that way at all, and his fear
was that she knew it also. He drew away from her
guiltily, covering his confusion by striding quickly
toward the door. "Good night," he said abruptly,
not looking at her.

He came back up the hall to Dr. Drew's room,
finding it lighted. This room had been Lars Thorson's own, and Tod had insisted that Drew take it.
There was a four-poster bed, broad and big, a
dresser, a scattering of chairs, and the pelt of a

mountain lion sprawled on the floor. Standing here, Thorson could sense something of his father's personality in this room, and he felt the loss of the years the two of them hadn't shared.

He was staring with eyes that did not see when Drew's voice brought him from his reverie.

Drew said, "I suppose we ought to go tell Zeke Lockhart that O'Doone is still in the diggings. But I doubt if it would do much good. O'Doone's probably well under cover after what happened."

"That's true," Thorson agreed. "Rory will keep till he shows himself again. And I've things to tell you." Whereupon he related his talk with Matthew Fee in the man's office over the Hurdy-Gurdy House and went on to tell of what had happened in the *Trumpet* building. "We can check the damage in the morning," he finished. "From what little I could see tonight, the press wasn't hurt much. But the paper stock's ruined. I wonder if Ginny realized that. We can't put out a paper on nothing."

Dr. Drew stroked his Imperial. "The pieces are beginning to fit into place, Tod," he said. "You're worrying Matthew Fee. In fact, you worried him even before you came here. It was common knowledge that you were on the way; I learned that out at the discovery claim tonight. Hazzard has had a crew working the claim, pending our arrival, and those muckers knew you were due any day. Was that why Rory O'Doone was waiting on top of Wolverine Pass?"

Thorson shrugged.

"Fee boosted you into the marshal's office in order to save his face today," Drew went on. "Also, he thought you might take it as a friendly act and unwittingly play hand-in-glove with him. When the two of you faced cards tonight, he found out how mistaken he was. Also he learned that you intended using the *Trumpet* against him. The fact that you

were in the building when he came to burn it was all
the better. You're a marked man now, Tod. He
knows that killing you is the only way to stop you
from taking up where Lars Thorson and Jamieson
Hazzard left off."

"I'll try to take a lot of killing," Thorson said.

Dr. Drew hesitated, patently choosing his words
with care. "We're men," he said, "and we can talk
to each other man-to-man. There's a time to be he-
roic, Tod, and a time when bravery can be foolish."

Thorson remembered that Ginny had voiced that
same thought earlier tonight, at the time when he'd
asked her to let him stay in Hazzard's quarters. He
said, "Meaning, Doctor—?"

"I can oversee the working of the discovery
claim," Drew said. "And if there's ever a way to get
the gold out of the gulch past those confounded
road agents, I can deposit your share of the income
in any bank you name. There's no real reason why
you have to stay here and stop a slug some dark
night."

Thorson turned that over in his mind, feeling no
resentment at the suggestion.

"I don't think the odds are so great as all that,
Doctor," he said.

Drew smiled. "Very well, Tod. The thought
crossed my mind that your main reason for staying
here might be for my sake, to help see that our claim
was properly worked. But you're Lars Thorson's
son, and the Viking's way is your way."

Thorson shook his head. "Fee told me tonight that
I wasn't half as big as Lars. He was right."

Drew nudged the mountain lion pelt with his toe.
"I'm wondering if this was the cat that Lars Thorson and I met in the Sierras many years ago," he
said. "It would have been like Lars to have toted
that hide all these years. You've heard the story behind it?"

"Lars came to St. Louis when I was a little shaver and told me the tale. And he showed me the scars on his chest. I know that he saved your life."

"We were camped just below the timberline," Drew explained. "Lars was looking for color, and I'd come along to keep him company. The cougar was on the limb of a tree overhanging our camp, and when he leaped, he landed squarely on top of me. He'd mauled me quite badly when Lars got his rifle to his shoulder, and it was a devil of a time for a gun to jam! But Lars had a hunting knife. He dragged that cat off me, and what happened then is something I'll remember to my grave. It was magnificent and it was terrible. I was just clinging to the ragged edge of consciousness, and I'd have given Lars one chance in a hundred to come through alive. When it was over, Lars was clawed to ribbons and the cougar was dead. A prospector found us later that day, though I don't remember that. Lars was three months on a hospital cot; I was five."

Thorson toed the lion's pelt. "It must have been some show."

"I haven't made my point plain," said Drew. "It was the spirit of Lars Thorson that counted—the Viking's way of going up against any sort of fight and coming through chiefly because he didn't know how to quit. I think you've got Lars' own magnificent stubbornness, Tod. And I think that Matthew Fee's sway in Thunder Gulch ended when you rolled in."

Thorson grinned broadly. "What were you saying about a time when bravery can be foolish?"

Dr. Drew smiled. "I hope you'll forgive me for that," he said. "And tomorrow we'll look over our claim together."

"Tomorrow," Thorson promised and bade Dr. Drew a grave goodnight.

Chapter Eight
BLOOD ON THE TRAIL

To walk through the ramifications of the Thunder Gulch diggings was to walk across the span of the centuries, for here was a panorama of all the means of mining from the primitive Mexican *batea*, or wooden bowl, to crude but comparatively modern attempts at hydraulic work. The western end of the gulch was given over to a maze of claims, and the draws and canyons biting into the slopes were yielding riches as well. Men were everywhere, a colorful swarm possessed of that most irresistible fever which has ever cursed the race—the lust for gold.

There were graybeards who had worked with pick and shovel and pan out of Sacramento and Yerba Buena and Placerville, and who worked with pick and shovel and pan still, scorning newer innovations with the die-hard stubbornness of their breed. There were men who toiled over rockers and sluices, wherever there was a fall of water. Others "gophered" under the slopes, pitting their brawn and their sweat in a gamble that they'd find a vein worth uncovering. In some places steel pipes, with monitors at the end, sent forth a jet of water to knife away some shouldering bank and bare the riches beneath it. And there were quartz mines too; shafts sunk deep into the earth with fingering tunnels from whence came tons of rock that would later be crumbled beneath the smashing force of a stamp mill.

Into this hurly-burly came Tod Thorson and Dr. Huntley Drew on their second afternoon in Thunder Gulch, making their inspection of the discovery claim and finding upwards of twenty men working the sluices under the direction of a brawny, red-faced Celt who'd been hired by Jamieson Hazzard to oversee the work till the heirs arrived.

This man, Pat Shea, was told that he could continue in his present capacity, for neither Thorson nor Drew laid any claims to being mining men, and they could use the skill of Shea.

Their inspection completed, the partners went on up the gulch to the adjoining claim of Zeke Lockhart where that worthy diligently poured water into a rocker while a short, swarthy French Canadian fetched pay dirt from the creek bank to dump into the contraption.

Thorson, his clothes torn in that fight in the *Trumpet* building, had discarded his dressy garb of yesterday. He wore a sombrero, the flannel shirt of a miner, and boots and breeches, and he'd found a six-shooter that had belonged to Lars Thorson and it was belted against his hip. Lockhart measured him for a long moment without recognition, then the gentle-eyed miner wiped his hand against his hip and extended it. "Howdy," he said. "Looking things over?"

Thorson nodded, glancing toward the Canuck and remembering him from the miners' court and the funeral. "Your partner?" he asked.

The swarthy one gave him a flash of white teeth and said, "Me, I am lend the helping hand. My claim, she is further up ze gulch and she is petered out. But me, Gaston Thiebault, I use ze sluices and she is dust, not ore, zat I've got hid away. When ze sign is right, m'sieu, I leave zeze damn' diggings."

Lockhart cast a quick glance around him. "You talk that way, and you'll have every road agent in the gulch watching for you to leave!"

Thiebault lifted his shoulders in a careless shrug. "You are my frien', by gar! And zeze are ze son and ze frien' of Lars Thorson. Zey keep my secret. Lars Thorson, she tell me, 'You file on zat claim, Frenchy, you get rich damn' queek.' " He pointed up-canyon with his finger. "By gar, she is right too! I am not afraid to trust ze frien's of Lars Thorson."

Hands were shaken all around, and Lockhart indicated the dark mouth of a nearby quartz shaft and said, "Some men have managed to get back to the states with their wealth. That's Tom Conway's old mine. He worked it out and ran the road agent gantlet with his ore, and he's getting fat on St. Louis food right now. Maybe Frenchy can do the same. But the whole gulch knows he's finished his work here and is waiting his chance. It's bad . . . bad."

Thiebault was more optimistic. "I fool zem," he declared. "Zey t'ink Thiebault she will take ze road to Fort Benton and go down ze Missouri, ze short way. Instead I go west, m'sieus, and soon. I make ze sneak by night to Lewiston, zen down ze Columbia and catch ze boat." He kissed his fingertips and waved toward them. "Someday I send you ze postcard from Paris where I am drink ze champagne from ze ladies' slippers!"

But Zeke Lockhart shook his gray head and Thorson saw him then as a symbol of all these men who were afraid and who toiled and ate and slept beneath the black and constant shadow of the road agent menace. And he remembered how many he'd met at Jamieson Hazzard's funeral and the estimate he'd placed upon their combined might. He said, "Good luck to you, Thiebault. Hope I see you again before you leave."

He went on, Dr. Drew with him, and the yawning mouth of Tom Conway's deserted shaft intrigued Thorson. "Think I'll have a look," he said and climbed down a ladder some twenty feet while Drew waited above. A tunnel ran from the bottom of the shaft, but it was too dark to explore more than briefly, and Thorson soon came aloft again. "There are rooms giving off the tunnel," he told Drew.

"Powder rooms and such. Matt Fee found it funny that Thunder Gulch had no jail. But Tom Conway's mine would make a good one if we needed a jail in a hurry."

"We'll remember it," Drew remarked.

They were nearly to the end of the diggings now, but a turn of the gulch gave them a view of another field of operation where a different race toiled. These were claims that had been defaulted by men who'd wrested a full share of riches from them, then gone out of Thunder Gulch to Salt Lake or Fort Benton or to death along the trail. And into these discarded claims had come the Chinese, those strange, adopted citizens of the West. Where the white man had shrugged, finding further returns not worth the effort, John Chinaman had, by diligent toil and painstaking effort, eked out a living from ground given up as barren.

They were everywhere, these yellow men, alike in their shapeless jackets and baggy trousers, many with bamboo poles across their shoulders from which hung the tools of this trade they'd taken over. Dr. Drew looked at them and smiled. "It's like seeing the California diggings all over again," he said.

Thorson had spied the one who interested him, that yellow, half-blind patriarch, Quong Lee, who worked a rocker near an anemic creek. Striding toward the man, he said, "Good afternoon, Quong. Remember me—Tod Thorson? I'm having my first look at the diggings."

Quong Lee turned his dimmed eyes toward the pair of them and gravely said, "Is good. Welcome. Our poor efforts bear scanty fruit, but you may find much to interest you."

Thorson nodded, wondering about this man whose speech held none of the singsong monotony of his people, and who arranged his words as a woman might arrange a cluster of flowers. His first meeting with Quong Lee, the introduction at Hazzard's funeral, had been brief. Even then he'd sensed that Quong Lee was no coolie, drawn from a far land to do lowly tasks for men who presumed to be his betters. He said, "Dr. Drew is with me. I don't believe you met him last night."

Quong Lee made a half-bow. "Name is recalled with honor," he said. "In California it was covered with greatness. I am humble in your presence."

"Then you know of the work the vigilantes did down there," Thorson said. "Do you think the same sort of an organization is needed here?"

"Is certain. My people suffer, too, from road agent doings. Happy day when law comes to Thunder Gulch. Would do all in my poor power to speed that day."

"I thought so," Thorson said.

They tarried only briefly after that, and when they went back up the gulch, Dr. Drew said, "I think I know what you were driving at, Tod. The Chinaman was sort of an alien outsider in the California days, but we've come to realize that he's as much a part of the West as any of us. If we organize vigilantes here, you'd like to include them?"

"Why not? I've had that notion ever since I met Quong Lee. They have the strength of numbers, and they've got a grudge against the road agents too."

"Quong especially," Drew remarked. "I happen to know something of his story. Heard it from Hazzard in the old days. A bunch of drunken ruffians decided to raid the Chinese diggings out of Sierraville one night. They figured the yellow boys would have gold worth grabbing, and they also intended having fun terrorizing them. They brought along blasting powder and set it off in a cluster of shacks. That's how Quong Lee nearly lost his eyesight—and his life. He was caught on the fringe of that blast. Afterwards the vigilantes managed to recover most of the dust that was stolen that night, and they returned it to the Chinese. I don't suppose Quong has forgotten any part of that episode."

"Probably not," Thorson agreed.

Most of this day was done when they came back to the camp, and Dr. Drew turned off at the trail to the stone house, murmuring something about having letters to write. Thorson went on to the *Trumpet* building. He'd looked it over this morning, along with Ginny, and he'd put men to work repairing the damage of the fire. These men were just quitting for the day when he came into the office. Ginny was here, soot-begrimed but smiling.

"We're not so crippled as I feared," she announced. "Thanks to the quick work of the bucket brigade, the press was hardly damaged. And type doesn't burn. Our paper supply is ruined, though, but it was pretty low anyway."

"More coming?" Thorson asked.

"Pi put in an order quite a while ago. It will come up from Salt Lake to Shoshone and over the Wolverines. Six-Hoss McNair, an independent freighter, will haul it in. But you can guess how long some supplies are in coming. It may be here before the week's out; it may be days longer."

He shrugged. "Supposing we go ahead and get the next edition set up anyway," he suggested. "If the paper comes, we'll run it off. If not, we'll just skip an issue or two until we can go to press again."

It was agreed, and there were busy days ahead for Thorson. While men toiled at repairing the building, their saws and hammers making a bedlam that had to be shouted down, Thorson learned the rudiments of the printer's trade from Ginny. Their hours were long together, and sometimes a self-conscious restraint lay between them, and he wondered if the memory of the night he'd kissed her was the cause of it.

They went to the stone house each evening and told Dr. Drew of the day's doings, and he promised them an editorial from his own pen when they would be ready for it.

On one of these days, almost a week after Thorson had come to Thunder Gulch, he saw Matthew Fee again. The man was riding up the gulch in a handsome rig, an open-topped buggy drawn by a spanking team of bays. An elegantly gowned woman rode with him, the flamboyant cut of her dress identifying her as one of the hurdy-gurdies. When she tipped her parasol, Thorson saw that she was Belle Kincaid. Instinctively he hoisted his sombrero, and she gave him a nod, but afterwards he was to wonder if she were worth the gallantry he'd bestowed.

He saw her again, that very night. He came into the Hurdy-Gurdy House, intending to do no more than have a quick look around, for his glimpse of Matthew Fee that day had reminded him of the showdown that had been postponed the night of the fire. If Fee was of a mind to take up the challenge he'd made, Thorson was of a mind to give him the opportunity. But Fee was nowhere about. The floor was thronged with dancers and the little Canuck, Thiebault, whirled past in the arms of Belle Kincaid. Thorson nodded to him and turned to go, but at that moment the music ceased and Thiebault came after him, clutching his arm.

"You have ze drink with me, m'sieu," he urged. "By gar, I buy you ze best zis house have!"

From the looks of him, Gaston Thiebault had had more drinks than one man could conveniently carry, but because he liked this easygoing Canuck, and because it was easier to accept than to argue with the man, Thorson nodded. They crossed to the bar together, and Thiebault made good his promise to "buy ze best zis house have."

"Mud in your eye," Thorson said and hoisted his glass.

"To your ver' good health, m'sieu," said Thiebault and lifted his own drink, but he did a neat job of spilling it on the floor and he winked ponderously at Thorson and gave him a flash of his white teeth.

"I do not mean ze offense by offering ze toast, zen not drinking ze drink," Thiebault said, low-voiced. "I am being ze fox, by gar. I make ze great show of drinking, and ze people say, 'Damn, zat Frenchy is on one grand toot. Tonight he sleep like ze grizzly b'ar in ze winter time, and tomorrow his head is so beeg he can't get it out ze door of his cabin!'"

He jerked at a rawhide thong stretched across his shirt, and a handsome gold watch appeared at the end of it. Snapping open the case, he eyed the watch owlishly. "Two, t'ree hours, m'sieu, and I am on ze trail to Lewiston. You see how I fool ze road agents?"

Thorson grinned. "Have another," he said and bought a drink that Thiebault dribbled down the front of his shirt. Thorson clapped him on the back. "Don't forget that postcard from Paris," he said.

Half an hour later Tod Thorson was bedded down in his room in the stone house, and he remembered Gaston Thiebault. He'd never see the little Canadian again, he knew, but the memory of him was something to cherish, and he fell asleep wondering how far Thiebault was along the trail. But he was to see Thiebault on the morrow, but not in the manner that he wished.

There was quite a crowd milling in the center of the street when Thorson and Ginny came toward the *Trumpet* building, and the center of that maelstrom was a shaggy prospector and a sleepy burro who'd come in from the West. Zeke Lockhart and Pat Shea and Josh Hoskins were in the crowd, and the prospector was telling a tale of blood and vio-

lence in a high-pitched excited voice. His words
were enough to send Thorson and others to saddles
and up the gulch to its farthest end, and beyond it
where the trail snaked through scattered timber
toward distant Idaho and the Lewiston diggings.
And here they found Gaston Thiebault.

A shotgun had cut down the Frenchman, and
there was blood on the trail where Thiebault had
managed to drag himself to one side to claw the
earth and die. The shotgun had made a mess of him,
and his pockets were turned inside out. Someone
found his horse and pack animal nearby, but they
were carrying nothing of value. Not now.

Tod Thorson stood looking upon this man who
would never go to Paris and drink champagne from
a lady's slipper, and he remembered Thiebault's
ruse that somehow hadn't worked, and a great
wrath grew within him and found its echo in the
muttered curses of the men around him.

One said, "And they got *him*, the poor little devil.
They got Frenchy and they got his gold. Damn' the
stinkin' sons! He never did nothing but good!"

Thorson looked at the little group and knew there
were none here he couldn't trust, and he raised his
hands. "Listen to me, gents," he said. "Listen close.
You all know Tom Conway's old deserted quartz
mine. Come there tonight, and bring along any man
who's proved himself honest. This is the last time a
man will ever leave Thunder Gulch to spill his blood
along the trail. We've got to see to that!"

Chapter Nine
OATH IN DARKNESS

They came out of the night with its nameless dread and met in the deeper darkness of an old abandoned quartz mine. They came furtively, skulking through the shadows, pausing often and straining their ears lest the crunch of their boots be echoed by the footfalls of others—others who'd wish to know what kept honest men from their beds, and who might follow to find out. They came when midnight's mantle spread velvety and awesome over the diggings. They knew the gravity of this thing they were about to do, for they were to be the first vigilantes of Thunder Gulch.

There were only a dozen in all. Tod Thorson was one, Dr. Drew another. Arriving earliest and fetching lanterns with them, they'd taken over the first room they found in Tom Conway's mine—a timber-shored dugout just off the main tunnel, a room that had once been used to store tools and which was littered with the debris of its former occupancy. The pair was waiting when the others dribbled in by twos and threes—Zeke Lockhart and Pat Shea and a half-dozen of their hardrock breed. Josh Hoskins, the stage driver, came, and so did Quong Lee, shaking off the helpful hands that might have guided him down the shaft and tunnel. Why should a man who'd spent half his life in shadows fear the darkness?

When they were assembled, seating themselves on discarded boxes and anything else that might support them, Thorson counted noses and said, "We're not many, but it's as good a turnout as I'd expected, at that. I won't waste words getting started. You know what happened last night, and why we're here. Thiebault is the second man we've buried in a week. We've got to organize, or the trails will be safe for no man. The vigilante idea is old to some of you, new to others. My partner, Dr. Drew, helped form such an outfit in California. I'm asking him to speak."

The lanterns, laying a pattern of somber shadows and yellowish light, made them a queer-looking crew, giving a ghastly cast to their strained faces, and when Dr. Drew arose, he might have been Mephistopheles until he began to speak.

"Most of my life has been spent in the forgotten corners of the world," he said. "Yet I've seen many a mining camp in my day. Some are overgrown with weeds now, deserted and forgotten. Some have become cities. And those, my friends, are the alternate destinies that Thunder Gulch faces. Lars Thorson dreamed that this camp would blossom into something lasting. Jamieson Hazzard tried to carry on that dream. Both of them are dead."

He paused, giving emphasis to his point, and then he said, "The stage that brought me into this camp also carried a man named Ed Folinsbee, a whiskey salesman, I believe. After a certain incident en route, I heard him swear that he'd get out of the camp as quickly as he could. Hoskins, you heard him. And I've learned that Folinsbee isn't the only man who prefers to give us a wide berth. I'm told that there isn't a single competent medico in all Thunder Gulch. The last one left weeks ago, after finding his cabin ransacked.

"I'm wondering, gentlemen, if this will always be a town that people will shun. And that, as I see it, depends on which of two factions rises to ascendancy. First, there are the people who come to seek gold and stay to build homes, the men who'll rear families and who will want to see a real city come out of the muck of these diggings. Gaston Thiebault might have been such a man. But Thiebault chose to leave the gulch, and he died in his attempt. Thiebault could see no future here. And why?

"Because there is a second faction that always comes on the heels of the first—the men who seek quick and easy riches, the desperadoes who prefer a land beyond the law, the gamblers, the hurdy-gurdies, and the other parasites. That, gentlemen, is the element which is growing stronger in Thunder Gulch every day. And that is why every honest man chooses to leave this place forever, if he dares, once his claim is worked.

"Thus our problem resolves itself into simple terms. If we are to have a lasting town, we must first have law. And we must organize our own. That's why we're here tonight. I know that most of you came hesitantly—and I don't blame you. We who stand together will be marked men, fighting an up-hill fight until our strength is great enough to over-awe the enemy. But I don't think that any man who signs up tonight will have cause to regret it.

"If some of you are not concerned with the future good that may come to Thunder Gulch out of our efforts, think of the present. I am told that you are hoarding your dust and your ore, not daring to take it over the trails. Organized and armed, we can send our own treasure trains across the Wolverines without paying Matthew Fee's price for freighting. And his hirelings won't dare try stopping us when we join together in our might to protect our own. That's all I have to say, gentlemen. I'd like to know how the rest of you feel about our plan."

He sat down in the midst of a solemn silence, and no ripple of applause came to break it, yet Thorson, looking around that grave semicircle of faces, knew that these men had been deeply impressed. Zeke Lockhart nodded and rose to speak for the rest. He

said, "You've told us what we need and why we
need it, Drew, and you said it good and plain. But
you also pointed out that there may be trouble for
those of us who join up first. I'm wondering how
we're going to gather the strength to make ourselves
felt."

"We've thought about that," Thorson said.
"Maybe we've got the answer. We can get recruits
by spreading the word from mouth to mouth, but
there's a faster way. The *Thunder Gulch Trumpet*
will push our organization. You see, I've less to
worry about than any of you. I've been a marked
man since the day Matt Fee fixed me up with a marshal's badge, then found out I wasn't going to use it
the way he thought."

"You mean the paper will announce that the vigilantes are here?"

Thorson nodded. "Oh, it won't say how strong or
weak we are, or who's in the outfit. But we'll let the
camp know that we've got a start and that we're
looking for members. I think it will put heart in a lot
of men. And I reckon that those who are interested
will read between the lines and come and see me to
learn how they can join up."

"It's a good idea," Lockhart decided. "A damn'
good idea!"

"You'll find the next issue of the paper interesting," Thorson promised. "Though it may be de-
layed. The fire took our paper stock, but we've more
coming overland. As soon as it gets here, we'll put
out an edition that should stir up a fuss."

"Then," said Lockhart, "there's nothing more to
do tonight but organize."

Dr. Drew produced pen, ink, and paper. "I've
drawn up some rules and regulations patterned after the California organization's. And we'll need an
oath."

"I was in the vigilantes over at Bannack," Lockhart said. "I haven't forgotten their oath, or their ceremony of taking the oath, and it should do for us. Write it down, if you want."

It was agreed, and one by one they affixed their names to the paper Dr. Drew had prepared, and after that was over the lanterns were extinguished and they stood in total darkness, here in this forgotten tunnel beneath the diggings, making a circle with their hands uplifted and repeating after Lockhart the oath of the first organization that had brought law to Montana:

"We, the undersigned, uniting ourselves together for the laudable purpose of arresting thieves and murderers and recovering stolen property, do pledge ourselves on our sacred honor, each to all others, and solemnly swear that we will reveal no secrets, violate no laws of right, and never desert each other or our standards of justice, so help us God."

It was highly theatrical, that oath in darkness, but it had been the foundation for law in another corner of this wild land, and it served the purpose of these men of Thunder Gulch. After it was over, they left the lanterns extinguished and climbed the ladder to the surface. Here they shook hands quickly and dispersed into the night, a dozen united men walking less furtively than before. And Tod Thorson, striding along with Dr. Drew toward the stone house and the girl who waited for them, said, "We've made a start. At least we've made a start! But until there's a dozen times a dozen of us, I hope, for the sake of the others, that our secret is safe."

But there'd been a thirteenth man at that first meeting of Thunder Gulch's vigilantes. He, too, had found an odd purpose for Tom Conway's deserted mine, and he'd slept in a shadowy heading for many nights now. He was there, bedded down on a litter of moldy blankets, when Dr. Drew and Thorson had first come with their lanterns, and they'd have found him if they'd had time and a need for a thorough exploration of the many tunnels. As it was, they'd not suspected that another might be in these musty depths, and thus they'd had no inkling of the presence of Rory O'Doone.

He'd chosen this mine for a hiding place, had Rory, for the same reason that Thorson had selected it for a meeting. Tom Conway had long since wrested all the riches from it, and the mine held no interest for the people of the diggings. A man with reason to keep under cover was safe here—or so O'Doone had presumed. And he was sleeping blissfully in the darkness when the thunder of boots awoke him this night to a realization that his sanctuary had been invaded.

Rory came out of his blankets in a cold sweat then, feeling for his guns and buckling them on, debating the merits of flight and fight and finding neither prospect any too attractive. Fight was out of the question. The sounds in the cavern indicated that the odds were too great for that. Nor was fleeing feasible, not with men blocking the ladder to the surface. It was, Rory O'Doone decided, the devil's own predicament.

He might have hunkered in the darkness, hoping that whoever had come would shortly go their way, but a great curiosity began to build in him, and he had to know who was here—and why. He hadn't pulled on his boots, so he eased his great bulk erect and cautiously slid one foot ahead of the other, coming down the tunnel as slowly as possible. It wasn't long until he was into the main tunnel, and seeing the splash of light from the tool room. Sucking in his breath, he was mindful of every rock that might rattle beneath his tread.

Dr. Drew was making his speech when Rory eased near the door. He heard enough of it to grasp its meaning, and he heard the remarks of Zeke

Lockhart and Tod Thorson afterward, and he was a silent witness to that oath in darkness that banded these men together. When they made talk of breaking up for the night, Rory took that as a cue, edging backward into the darkness that lay thick and heavy with the extinguishing of the lanterns. Men came groping out of the room toward the ladder, the crunch of their boots covering any slight sound Rory might have made in his eagerness to be gone before he was discovered.

The vigilantes ascended the ladder, talking among themselves as each awaited his turn to climb, and in this manner Rory was able to identify most of them. He turned their names over in his mind, one by one, eager to engrave them there, and he stood in the darkness for a long time after they'd gone, finding himself wet with perspiration. Indecisiveness had a heavy hand on him, partly because he couldn't be sure whether the vigilantes had parted or whether they were grouped at the top of the shaft. Finally he made his cautious way back to where he'd bedded, found his boots and tugged them on.

When he came into the main tunnel again, the silence was so thick that it was almost tangible, and when he reached the ladder and began climbing, he'd have sworn that it creaked loudly enough to wake every citizen of Thunder Gulch.

Reaching the surface, he paused, and if there'd been anyone to see, he might have judged, and rightly, that Rory O'Doone was scared. Tonight he had witnessed something so big and significant that he was possessed of a feeling of impotency and a compelling need to seek the company of his own kind and to be reassured by the sight of their strength. More than that, there was one who would want to know of this night's doings, one who might know the way to uproot the seed of the law before it sprouted.

Facing into the night, Rory O'Doone ran toward the distant Hurdy-Gurdy House of Matthew Fee. . . .

The next day was a busy one for Tod Thorson. He was at Jamieson Hazzard's desk shortly after dawn, and the copy that he scribbled off was passed to Ginny for her flying fingers to set into type. When the night came, the forms were finished, locked, and ready for the press that couldn't be fed. Ginny's work was completed first, and it was half an hour later that Thorson came up the gulch in the cool of the evening, and just before he turned to climb the trail to the stone house, he met Belle Kincaid.

Seeing her from a distance, tall and queenly, he remembered their first meeting in Josh Hoskins' stagecoach out of Shoshone and the estimate he had placed upon her resourcefulness at the time. In her way she'd been a riddle then, and she was more so now, and he'd tried in vain to understand her. She was a regular habitant of Fee's Hurdy-Gurdy House, an employee there, and she'd taken a cabin up the gulch. That much he knew. To his way of thinking, she had gone over to the enemy, and even though his attitude toward her might be tempered by tolerance and a certain inherent gallantry, he couldn't shake off some of his suspicions.

As she drew nearer he lifted his sombrero and said, "Good evening." She nodded in return, breaking her stride, and he sensed that she had something to say, though she continued holding silent. He fumbled awkwardly for words, then said, "I made you an offer of help, once. This is the first chance I've had to say that it's still open. You don't have to work where you do."

She forced a smile. "I'm not above dancing for a living," she said. "I've done it before. Most of us usually fall short of the mark we set for ourselves."

"But in Fee's place—?"

She shrugged. "The pay is good, and it may present other opportunities."

With little sleep the night before, this arduous day had put a sharp edge to his temper, and he didn't try to fathom her meaning before he said, "I shouldn't wonder! And that reminds me. Frenchy Thiebault spent a great deal of time with you the evening before he tried to sneak out of the diggings. Did he tell you that he planned on leaving? Or did you guess that his carousing was mostly pretense?"

It was as though he'd slapped her face, and when he saw the way she stiffened, he was ashamed of his words and wished he could reclaim them. She drew her shawl tightly about her shoulders, the knuckles of her right hand standing out starkly white. "So that's what you think!" she said. "You must hate me very much."

"No, I don't hate you," he said. "Maybe it would be better if I could."

She swept past him, then spun about. "You want no advice from me, I'm sure," she said. "Probably I'm a fool to risk giving you any. But walk softly, Thorson. Remember that. Walk softly, and watch your back, and tell your friends to do the same!"

She whisked away then, and Thorson looked after her and whistled softly and fumbled for tobacco. But he got no wisdom out of the cigarette he spun, and he could only promise himself that he'd ask her to explain her warning when next they met. But with the morning there was a new development that sent him on a dangerous trail and banished the thought of Belle Kincaid temporarily from his mind.

The man who was waiting when Thorson and Ginny came to the *Trumpet* office was browned by the winds of the high places and thick of sinew from hauling at a freight wagon's reins. Also he was bloody and disheveled, and he paced the street with a limp. He was Six-Hoss McNair, owner of the independent one-wagon freight outfit that had fought a valiant battle against Matthew Fee's monopoly. And the sight of him brought a stricken cry from Ginny even before Six-Hoss spoke.

"Yeah," the man said, "you guessed it. I've lost your supplies. I was coming down the slant of the Wolverine last night when half a dozen masked galoots jumped out of the bushes and hauled me off the wagon. I put up a fight and got pistol-whipped for my trouble. They shot my horses, set my wagon afire and tipped it over the edge of the slope. I come walking into camp this morning. I reckon that load of paper I was fetching for you is burned to ashes by now."

Thorson cursed and said, "I'm sorry for you, feller. And that little deal didn't do us any good either. What one fire failed to do, another finished!"

"It's the end of my outfit," Six-Hoss said. "And it's the end of my hopes in these diggings. Matt Fee's got it all now. And you can bet his wagons will have no trouble getting through. There were some behind me when I pulled out of Shoshone—wagons toting liquor for Matt Fee's bar and wallpaper for Matt Fee's walls. That's cargo that won't be stopped!"

"No?" said Thorson and saw the shape of a desperate idea born of the needs of a desperate situation. Then, without further word, he turned away, heading toward the livery stable which rented saddlers. Fifteen minutes later found him taking the trail. And as he put his back to Thunder Gulch and headed for the long slant up the Wolverines, he drew his forty-five from its holster, spun the cylinder and had a careful look at the loads.

Chapter Ten
TOD THORSON—ROAD AGENT

Out of Thunder Gulch the road snaked across a barren flat where a few latecomers, finding no claims for the taking in the diggings, scratched disconsolately. Beyond this stretch of desolation the twin ruts began to tilt upward, but here the trail forked, one branch, sage-grown and long-abandoned, pointing southward and vanishing into the gloomy mouth of a canyon, while the other, the regular stage road, climbed the slant of the Wolverines. The stage had brought Tod Thorson by this regular road the night of his arrival in the gulch, but the darkness had given him no view of his surroundings at that time. This, then, was strange country to him, but he had only to follow the climbing road, and he did, finding that the going smoothed out for a distance between each sharp pitch, and thus he ascended a giant's stairway toward the sky.

From the first of these straight stretches, he looked down upon Thunder Gulch, and the scatteration of tents and buildings and shacks, wrapped in the mists of morning, lost some of its sordidness viewed from this height. Pausing here, he could visualize the Thunder Gulch that would be when the fight was won, and his solemn speculation drew his lips tight and dissolved his last doubt as to whether he should do the thing he'd taken this trail to do. Then he was jogging his horse onward and upward, and a turn of the trail made a curtain between him and the camp.

To his left rose a sloping bank, bush-fringed at its bottom where chokecherry and rose briar and serviceberry rioted. To his right, always, the land

dropped away, sometimes so precipitously that following the road was skirting eternity, but sometimes that downsweeping pitch was so gradual that
a man could ride it if he chose. The canopy of sky
stretched above, and the mountaintop was lost in it.
Tod felt his smallness in this high and lonely land.

For the first few hours, he had the road to himself,
and it was easy to forget his mission under the spell
of all this grandeur. But when he heard the distant
creaking of a wagon, the ring of hoofs against rock,
he was recalled to reality. Dismounting and hauling
his horse into the bushes to the left, he looked to his
gun again, pulled his neckerchief up over his nose,
and tugged his sombrero lower, and he was this way
when the high-sided freight wagon rounded a turn
and came into view.

At this point the wagon was braked to the last
ratchet against the steep pitch of the trail, the driver
hauling against the reins of his six-span, and the
load was barely moving when Thorson stepped out
of the bushes. "Raise 'em!" he ordered briskly and
gestured with his gun.

The freighter might have been kicked by a mule.
Stunned for the moment, he gazed glassily at Thorson, then hoisted his hands. He said, "Mister, I
think you're making a helluva mistake!"

"Maybe," Thorson admitted and set his foot upon
the hub of a front wheel. Hauling himself up, he had
a look in the wagon, and since the crates were
plainly stenciled, he knew that the planing mill Matthew Fee had ordered was on its way. But this was
not the cargo Thorson sought, so he came down to
the ground again. "Move on," he told the driver.
"And don't look so pop-eyed. For all you know, I
might be one of Matt Fee's boys doing this just to
keep in practice."

The freighter cursed, but was eager enough to
obey, urging his horses to action and heading on

down the slant. Thorson watched the outfit round a turn, jerked his neckerchief from his face and mounted again. He was a mile up the trail when he heard a second wagon coming.

Into the bushes again, he quickly prepared to repeat his performance, smiling bleakly with the thought that he might be adept at road agent's art before this day was through. When he came into view and barked his brisk command, the second wagon stopped, its driver, a younger man than the first, betraying the same ludicrous astonishment.

"Just hold yourself steady, son," Thorson advised and climbed for a look. Whiskey was in this wagon, whiskey consigned to Matthew Fee's Hurdy-Gurdy House, but another commodity was being carried as well—wallpaper. Thorson had found the wagon he wanted, the one Six-Hoss McNair had seen in Shoshone.

"Pile down," he ordered the driver. "It's a long walk into Thunder Gulch, but it's all downhill. I'm taking over this outfit from here on."

"To hell with you!" snarled the driver and reached for the rifle he kept at his feet.

That gave Thorson little choice. He brought his gun barrel up and down again, catching the driver along the side of his head, and the fellow crumpled like a snowman in the sun, folding over limply and dropping the rifle he'd managed to reach. Thorson caught him before he toppled off the wagon and managed to ease him to the ground. Propping up the man at the side of the road, he looked him over and decided the driver would be awake before an hour ran out. Then Thorson tied his saddler to the tailgate of the wagon, climbed to the seat, took the reins in his hands and kicked off the brake.

So far, success had perched on his shoulders, but since two of Fee's wagons had been on the trail today, he was mindful that there might be others. If the driver he'd left behind hailed a Fee wagon when he recovered consciousness, there'd probably be an effort made to overtake the stolen wagon, and there might be gunplay. Therefore Thorson contrived to put the miles behind him, letting the horses stretch out wherever the road ran even, and not crowding the brake too hard on the slopes. And in midafternoon he overtook the wagon ahead of him, the one he'd first stopped.

This was another contingency Thorson had anticipated, for hurrying to outdistance any wagon that might be behind him had, of necessity, meant that sooner or later he'd overhaul the one ahead. But luck favored him; the road was steep at this point, but it was wide as well. The wagon with the planing mill was crawling along, its brake squealing, and Thorson, putting a quick and accurate reckoning on the situation, saw his only course.

Kicking off his brake, he slapped the wheel horses with the reins. Instantly the huge wagon was rolling downward, the horses crowded into a gallop by the press of the load behind them. They came down that slant like something catapulted, the wheels flicking gravel over the edge of the rim. With the wagon ahead crowded as far to the right as possible, Thorson had no choice but to take the outside.

Streaking past the other wagon, Thorson had a blurred glimpse of the astonished face of its driver. The man shouted, but the wind howling past Thorson's ears deafened him, though he heard the rifle bang. Casting a glance to the rear, he saw the freighter with a gun cradled to his shoulder, and he knew that the man had recognized him from their first meeting and was going to make a fight. Thorson's own gun swung at his hip, and the rifle that the driver of this wagon hadn't been able to use was within reach. But he had to keep his hands on the reins.

A curve was ahead, and a handful of seconds would put him around it. But he felt fire along his ribs, the smash of lead almost tearing him off the wagon. He grasped at the seat with one hand, gritting his teeth against the savage force of the pain. He had a spinning glimpse of space and a tangled jungle of pine tops below him, but he was holding firmly as his wagon swept around the turn and beyond the reach of the rifle.

Still he kept to this killing pace, for if the man behind him chose to make a race of it, there'd be other straight stretches where that rifle could do its work. Thorson's gamble was that the man wouldn't risk any such wild riding on this steep slant, and he took curve after curve, pitting his strength and his skill against the trail. Then, satisfied that he'd safely outdistanced the man behind him, he began using the brake again.

Also he looked to his wound. The bullet had no more than raked his ribs, but he'd shed enough blood to feel the loss. Fashioning a crude bandage from his undershirt as he drove along, he had it tied into place when he came across the desolate flat toward Thunder Gulch at the day's end. Deep darkness was beginning to settle, and he attracted no attention in the teeming camp where a dozen wagons strove for right of way. Thus he was able to bring his cargo surreptitiously to the rear of the *Trumpet* building.

He hadn't realized how weak he was until he came down off the wagon. When he stepped toward the door, a wave of nausea made the ground unsteady, and he put his hand to the wall for support, knocking feebly and reeling on his feet till the door opened and Ginny found him.

"Tod!" she cried. "There's blood on you! You're hurt!"

Just to hear the concern in her voice made his

hurt worth the having. She led him inside the building, easing him into a chair in the press room and
beginning to strip his shirt away, and he marveled
that she asked no questions, giving all her attention
to his wound instead. She bustled into Hazzard's
former quarters, returning with boiling water, and a
bedsheet which she tore into strips.

"I'll have to get some whiskey to bathe the
wound," she said.

"You'll find a wagon load of it out behind," he
murmured.

She came back bent beneath the weight of a case
of whiskey, quickly opened it and smashed the head
from a bottle against the press. He took a long pull
at the liquor, and she used the rest on the wound,
and while she worked he told her what he'd done.

She said, "But I don't understand. What will we
do with those things?"

"We can wallpaper the town, if we want to. I've
just stolen a page from Matthew Fee's own book."

Her eyes lighted and he liked that. "But, Tod, you
shouldn't have run such a risk!"

"Does it matter to you?" he asked, and she made
no answer, but suddenly he knew that it did matter
to her and he was humbled by the knowledge. With
her bending to bandage him, he could smell the elu-
sive perfume of her hair, and he fell to wondering
how many men had paid court to her and he decided that he hated all of them. When she finished
her work, he had another pull at a whiskey bottle
and felt equal to the work that was yet to be done.

Together they unloaded half of Fee's cargo, moving it into the building, and while they busied themselves he asked, "That old road that turns to the
right just beyond the flats? Where does it lead?"

"The Old South Road?" she said. "It runs to Shoshone, but it's the long way and rough going and it

hasn't been used since they put a road over Wolverine Pass. Why?''

"Fee may come looking for his wagon," Thorson said. "I don't want him to find it here."

She made him eat before he left, and he was whole enough to be ready for anything when he climbed to the wagon seat once again. Picking his way out of the camp, he tooled the wagon through the night, crossing the flat and taking the fork to the south when he came to it. Following this abandoned road for a mile or so into the canyon, he began to understand why the trail was no longer used. The going was indeed rough, and several times he had to lead the horses around rocky outcroppings. There was a moon by the time he came as far as he intended, and by its light he cut the horses from their harness and scattered them with a wave of his sombrero. Then he untied his saddler from behind the wagon, climbed into the kak, and the shadows claimed him as he headed back toward Thunder Gulch.

The descending night had found a half-dozen men far up that same canyon, and here a tiny fire made its feeble mark against the encroaching darkness. Within the rim of its light some of the men milled restlessly, the others crouched around a spread blanket, busy at a poker game. The man with the largest amount of winnings piled before him was Rory O'Doone, and his luck with the pasteboards had put him in a fine good humor.

He said, "What you buckos don't know about cards would fill a mighty big book. Who's got anything to ante besides his shirt?"

A bucktoothed man with a yellowish cast to his skin threw down his cards in disgust. "Sometimes I wonder how a man can be as lucky at poker as you, Rory," he said. "I've lost my share of the dust just about as fast as I made it."

Rory grinned, choosing to overlook the insinuation. "Lucky at cards, unlucky at love, that's me," he said. "You boys seen that new woman at Matt Fee's place? I'd hand you back your dust for an honest-to-God smile from her. But what kind of a chance has a man got when he can't show himself in camp without runnin' the risk of sticking his head in a noose?"

He of the buckteeth said, "So the Kincaid woman looks good to you, eh? What kind of fool is the boss to keep her around? She came out here to marry Pi Hazzard. Everybody knows that. She's just waiting a chance to knife Matt in the back."

"Doheny, you don't know any more about women than you do about cards," Rory scoffed. "Sure, she come to marry Hazzard. Why not? He was in thick with Lars Thorson, Lars owned the discovery claim, and Pi looked like a mighty good buy in the marriage market. But if she really gave a hoot about him, why didn't she marry him years back? They were supposed to be engaged in California. I was there, and I know. But how's it all worked out? Hazzard's dead; the good thing is gone. Matt Fee's the big auger hereabouts. She finds that out in a hurry, so she ties up with Matt. She's no fool."

He fell to picking up his winnings, mostly filled pokes of gold dust. These he stowed into his pockets. There was a handsome gold watch too, fastened to the end of a rawhide thong. "I'm heading in to see Matt," he said. "See you later, boys. Who knows? Maybe some other mouthy fool is ready to try sneaking out of the diggings with his dust."

Back in the shadows stood a cabin with a corral behind it. From this peeled-pole structure, O'Doone got his saddler, threw gear onto it and headed up the canyon with a farewell wave to his fellows. From long habit he held to the shadows and rode warily, and thus he heard the faint sounds of an approaching wagon from a safe distance. Coming down off his horse, he tied the animal in a thicket and began stealing forward on foot. Since the night before last when he'd been awakened in Tom Conway's deserted mine, no place had seemed quite safe to Rory O'Doone. That was why he meant to find out who was using an abandoned trail leading straight to a road agent hideout.

The sound of the wagon ceased, and that made him more curious than ever. When he saw it bulking ahead, there was moonlight enough to recognize it, and since it was Matthew Fee's, Rory's first thought was that Fee was sending supplies to the shebang. But the man clambering down from the wagon seat was going about the business of cutting the horses from their harness, and that made no sense. Then the man turned, and O'Doone had a glimpse of his face, recognizing Tod Thorson instantly. He sucked in a long breath, did Rory, and his gun came into his hand and leveled, and a string drawn from the barrel to the heart of Thorson would have had no slackness in it.

The thing that saved Thorson's life was the consuming curiosity of Rory O'Doone. He had to know what Thorson was up to, so he held his trigger finger lax as Thorson went to the rear of the wagon. A scraggly fir laid a somber shadow, and Thorson was lost in it until he was up into a saddle and heading along the back trail. Thus did Rory miss his chance at the kind of shot he'd have liked, and the memory of the gun-skill Thorson had displayed atop Wolverine Pass was strong enough to stay Rory's finger after that.

As the rataplan of hoofs died in the distance, Rory eased to the wagon, had a look at its cargo and sandpapered his blocky chin with his fingers, putting a speculation upon all this and finding that it fitted into no reasonable pattern. He had an urgent need for a wiser head, so when he went back to his saddler and mounted, he was more anxious than ever to see Matthew Fee. He came up the canyon as cautiously as before, mindful that Tod Thorson was ahead of him, and he still kept to the shadows after he'd reached Thunder Gulch.

To the rear of the Hurdy-Gurdy House there was a covered stairway that brought Rory to the second floor and he strode down the hall quickly and entered the lavish office of Matthew Fee with no more than the ghost of a knock. Fee was here, sprawled in a plush-covered chair, a drink in his hand. Scowling, he said, "Rory, you damn' fool! You've got to quit busting into camp every time you get the notion. First you hid in Tom Conway's mine when you were supposed to be out of the gulch—though I'm mighty glad you did. But I've told you to lie low in the canyon till I sent for you. If it's that woman that's fetching you in, I'll fire her!"

Rory waved the reprimand aside. "Here's something as interestin' as what I heard down in the mine," he said. And he told his tale and Fee listened, his broad forehead corrugating before O'Doone had finished.

"You're sure it was Thorson, Rory?" Fee demanded.

"Dead sure."

"Joe Coulter brought in my planing mill tonight," Fee said. "He spun a wild yarn about being stopped by a road agent, then seeing the galoot streak past him on the slant with another of my wagons afterwards. Joe swears he creased the man with his rifle. He described the fellow, but it might have been any one of a hundred men. So it's Thorson who's taken to road agenting!"

"What do you make of it, boss?"

"I don't know," Fee admitted. "I'm damned if I know. But I'm wondering if Tod Thorson hasn't just dealt us the cards which will mean the end of his vigilante outfit when we play 'em. Help yourself to a drink, Rory, and don't bother me. I've got some thinking to do."

Chapter Eleven
TRIAL BY FURY

In the cool hours of early morning, Tod and Ginny were busying themselves in the *Trumpet* building when Zeke Lockhart dropped around. Greeting him, Thorson glanced at Lockhart's knees, saw no mud there and judged correctly that the man hadn't been working his claim today. Something was on Lockhart's mind, something that troubled him no little bit. Thorson could see that in the tight-lipped look of the man, and he encouraged him by saying, "Good morning, Zeke. On a bet, I'd guess you've got news for the paper."

"Wa-al, not exactly," Lockhart countered. He perched his thin frame on the edge of Hazzard's desk, picked up a pencil, fiddled with it indecisively and put it down. Then: "Tod, Matt Fee came to see me this morning. He tells a crazy tale, but it's one I can't laugh off. He says you stole one of his freight wagons yesterday, and he seems to have a sizable amount of proof to back him."

Thorson made no effort to hide his surprise, and he wondered how Matthew Fee had discovered the truth so quickly. "What does Fee want you to do about it?" he asked.

"He came to me because I'm head of the miners' court. He said he couldn't very well ask the town marshal to arrest himself, and he wants you put on trial."

Thorson shrugged. "Then it's simple enough. We'll oblige him. Am I under arrest meanwhile?"

Lockhart stared, astonishment unhinging his jaw. "Thorson, is there something to this?" he demanded. "When Fee came to me, my best guess was that he'd learned what we've been doing. I figured he was making a wild play to try and blacken your reputation in the diggings. But if he brings you to trial—!''

"—He makes a monkey out of me, or I make one out of him,'' Thorson finished. He laid his hand on Lockhart's shoulder. "Quit your worrying, Zeke. I expected this, but hardly so quick. Call your court together this afternoon.''

Lockhart said, "But he must have something to hang onto you, or he wouldn't want you put to trial.'' His gentle eyes widened. "Tod, there's no truth in his charge, is there?''

Thorson smiled. "After all, you'll be sitting in the judge's seat at the trial. It wouldn't be fair to tell you anything that might prejudice you. Now run along and get ready to ring your bell, Zeke. I'll come a-running when I hear it.''

Lockhart made his departure, obviously not one whit impressed by Thorson's surety, and after he'd gone, Ginny came to Tod, and her hands were tiny and ink-smudged against his shoulders. She said, "Tod, I'm scared!''

"Of what Matthew Fee's going to try and do? Don't be.''

"But this isn't St. Louis, Tod. You've never seen a miners' court trial. The head of the court is the judge, but there's no jury, and the temper of the crowd does the real deciding. Many a man has been dragged out and hanged before a trial was half over. It's trial by fury, that's what it is, and you can be sure that Fee will have all his own men there to stir the miners against you. Rory O'Doone was only banished for what he did, but that was because Zeke Lockhart had a tiger by the tail that day, and Zeke knew it. He'll try to protect you, but he won't be able to do much if the crowd gets out of hand. There was blood spilled yesterday, remember. Fee will play that up."

"It was my blood, wasn't it?" Thorson countered. But because her fear stood stark in her hazel eyes, he added gently, "Do you think I wasn't expecting something like this? Fee was bound to discover the truth eventually. But I had a plan in case he did. Listen and I'll tell you about it."

While he talked, he watched the change come over her, and he had her smiling before ten minutes ran out and laughing by the time he'd finished. "So you see, we've got a busy morning ahead of us," he concluded. "We'd better be at it."

After that Thorson began pacing the floor, dictating rapidly, and Ginny's nimble fingers set his words in type. Then the form for the paper's front page, locked and ready, was torn down and reassembled. Dr. Drew came in while they were doing this, and Thorson told him all he needed to know, and Drew gave his approval to the plan and lent a hand with the work.

They snatched a quick meal at noontime, Ginny cooking it in the kitchen Hazzard had used. They went back to work as quickly as they'd eaten, but there was still much to be done when the big bell atop the miners' court began to toll. Ginny looked up as Tod reached for his sombrero. "The doctor and I will be leaving now," Thorson said. "Think you can handle things alone?"

She came to him again, her hands against his shoulders. "I'll get along," she said. "Oh, Tod, be careful!"

He smiled a promise and went out the door, Dr. Drew with him, the pair striding along the gulch and climbing the trail toward the miners' court building. Many men were on that trail, men who swarmed from the diggings and from the town proper, and when Thorson and Drew came into the building, they found some of the plank seats already packed. Some had obviously come here even before the bell had been rung. Zeke Lockhart was on the raised platform at the end of the room, and he'd placed a table there and lined up the scattered chairs. Thorson looked at Lockhart and winked expansively, but his good humor wrung no like response from the head of the miners' court.

Matthew Fee was here, dressed as he'd been the other day he'd stood in this hall, his black coat stretched taut at the shoulders, his florid face wreathed in a smile. It was his cohorts who'd come early, and they sat massed together. Peering in the semidarkness, Thorson gauged their number and found it greater than he'd expected.

But friends of his were filtering in—Josh Hoskins and Pat Shea and miners who'd stood with him in darkness and repeated an oath. Quong Lee came too, a half-dozen Chinese with him, the Orientals taking a stand to the rear of the room. But it was the third element that interested Thorson—the miners of the gulch who owed no allegiance either to Fee or to himself and who might be a straw in the wind today. Such men had voted him a marshal's badge. Such men might as easily take it away and banish him from the boom-camp.

He wondered what the outcome of the trial would be, some of his surety fading with the thought that his scheme to checkmate Fee might be too feeble to accomplish its purpose, and he knew a gnawing impatience to get on with the trial and face the showdown. Zeke Lockhart was tasting that same uneasy tension, for he cleared his throat and rapped upon the table and said, "Those of you that don't know are wondering why you've been called here today. This is a trial. Matthew Fee's made a charge of road agenting against a citizen of the gulch."

Fee came to his feet, unbuttoned his coat and

thrust his thumbs into the pockets of his waistcoat. "That's right," he said. "I'm charging Tod Thorson with stealing one of my freight wagons."

A startled murmur swept through the assemblage, and Thorson came erect and spoke above the buzz of it. "Just how do you conduct one of these trials, Zeke?" he asked. "Am I allowed counsel?"

"We're not much on correct judicial procedure," Lockhart explained. "The accuser calls witnesses to support his claim. The accused can do the same. Either one of you can speak for yourself or be represented, if you'd rather. That satisfactory?"

Thorson nodded. "My friend, Dr. Drew, will represent me whenever he wishes."

Fee said, "You'll need more than a lawyer, bucko." He looked about the room. "Joe Coulter!" he called. "Gents, you all know Joe. He's my first witness."

The minute Coulter came to the front of the room, Thorson recognized him as the first man he'd stopped on the slant of Wolverine Pass, the one who'd later fired at him with a rifle. He heard Coulter sworn in as a witness, and he listened to the man's account of being held up, ordered to go on and afterwards passed by the road agent.

"He streaked by me like the devil was riding his shirttail," Coulter testified. "Sooner Dobbs had been behind me out of Shoshone with another of Matt's wagons, but I knew damned well it wasn't Sooner crowding his horses on a steep pitch. The minute I figgered it was the road agent driving Sooner's wagon, I reached for my rifle. Creased him too, I'm pretty sure, just before he rounded a turn and got out of sight."

Zeke Lockhart, looking more worried than ever, sent an inquiring glance at Thorson and said, "Any questions you want to put to the witness?"

Dr. Drew stood up, brushing a lock of hair from

his high brow. "Coulter, you testified that the road agent was masked with a bandanna when he stopped you. You said he wasn't masked when he passed you with the stolen wagon, but you also said he was going very fast. Can you swear that Tod Thorson was the man you saw?"

"Sure I can swear it! He's still wearing the same clothes he had on yesterday."

Drew glanced at Thorson. "Miner's garb," Drew scoffed. "You can find a hundred men dressed like him."

He nodded, dismissing Coulter, and as the man came down from the platform, Matthew Fee called Sooner Dobbs. Dobbs was the freighter Thorson had left unconscious beside the trail, and he was in a sullen mood and his testimony was liberally sprinkled with profanity. His story finished, Lockhart invited questions, and Thorson solemnly asked, "How did you get back to the diggings, Dobbs? Walk all the way—downhill?"

"Another wagon came along," Dobbs snarled. "It picked me up by the time I'd got my feet good and blistered!"

"That's too bad," Thorson said and looked at Lockhart. "Can I call a witness?"

When Lockhart nodded, Thorson looked for the man whose entrance he'd noticed earlier. "Six-Hoss McNair," he said.

The surprised freighter limped to the stand and was sworn in. Thorson said, "You run an independent freight outfit, I'm told. Will you tell what happened to you and your outfit when you were on your way into the gulch the night before last?"

McNair gave his story of violence on the trail and of a wagon ruined and a cargo destroyed. When he'd finished, Thorson asked, "Would you say that *I* was one of the road agents who stopped you?"

Matthew Fee waved his arms wildly. "This is

crazy!" he thundered. "What happened to McNair
and what happened to my outfit is two different
things. According to this freighter's testimony, he
was bringing in paper for the newspaper that Thorson is helping Ginny Drew run. Anybody with an
ounce of brains knows that he didn't go out and
destroy a cargo that just the same as belonged to
him! Proving that he was innocent of holding up
McNair doesn't prove him innocent of stealing my
wagon. He's trying to confuse the issue!"

Thorson bowed. "Fee, you've got the makings of a
first-class shyster," he said.

Lockhart dismissed McNair and faced the crowd
indecisively. "I can't see where anything's been
proved so far," Lockhart said. "A masked man
stopped Coulter, and that same masked man
stopped Dobbs. But where's the positive proof that
the masked man was Thorson? If this is all the evidence you've got, Fee, your accusation is a farce!"

"Is it?" Fee challenged. "It doesn't make sense,
eh, that the marshal of Thunder Gulch might be a
road agent. Yet some of you remember Bannack
where the sheriff who'd been duly elected by the
citizens turned out to be the head of the road agents
and was hanged for his crimes. The same thing
could happen here, and I think it has. I—"

A big man with buckteeth and a yellowish cast to
his skin came to his feet shouting. "Thorson's
crooked!" he cried. "Any man can see it! He's hiding behind the badge we pinned on him, but I'm
claiming he ain't even the man he pretends to be!
Look at him! Does he look like any son of Lars Thorson? He's wormed his way into this camp and
fooled us all, but it ain't too late to ride him out on a
rail!"

The crowd rumbled with one voice, a throaty,
primitive sound, and suddenly Thorson saw all the
intent of Matthew Fee, and he knew then, just as

surely as though the truth were tangible, that Fee
had learned of the organization of the vigilantes.
Belle Kincaid had known too, and she'd gotten her
knowledge from Fee. That was what had been behind her warning to Thorson and his friends to walk
softly. Fee had the truth, and Fee was out for blood.
When this trial was over, it wouldn't matter
whether Tod Thorson was banished from the gulch
or not. No man would come to join his vigilantes,
for no man would trust him. Matthew Fee meant to
see to that.

Ginny had called this a trial by fury, and that's
what Fee intended it to be, and he was playing his
cards with care. Waving his arms again, he was
shouting above the growing rumble of anger. "Gentlemen! Gentlemen!" he cried. "Thorson hasn't
been convicted yet. Give him a chance. And listen to
my next witness. *Rory O'Doone!*"

Not until then did Tod Thorson realize that Rory
O'Doone was here. The big man had sat in the midst
of Fee's followers, his sombrero tugged low, and
when O'Doone came to his feet, Thorson was as surprised as anybody. If fear and anger had marked
O'Doone's last appearance in this hall, surety and
satisfaction rode on his broad shoulders now. Grin-
ning widely, he came up the aisle to the witness
chair, took his oath and began speaking.

"Last night I was riding along the Old South
Road," he said. "I saw a jigger come driving toward
me with one of Matt Fee's wagons, and while I
watched, he got off and cut the horses out of their
harness and scattered 'em. Then he piled onto a saddler he had tied behind the wagon and loped back
toward the camp. There was moon enough to see
him, gents. It was Tod Thorson, and no mistake!"

The buck-toothed man began shouting again, others increasing the clamor, and Zeke Lockhart
rapped futilely for order. But above the roar, Dr.

Drew managed to make himself heard. "By what right does this man testify here?" Drew demanded. "He was banished from the diggings—banished by testimony of Thorson and myself, testimony which proved him a road agent! This is just a cheap attempt at revenge!"

Matthew Fee made answer. "Rory *left* the gulch," he insisted. "After all, the banishment didn't extend to the ends of the earth! Rory's been prospecting in the hills to the south. When he saw Thorson last night, he came to me and told me about it. I asked him to appear here today. As I see it, Rory has the right to clear himself, if it's possible. And he certainly deserves some consideration, seeing as how the man who accused him of being a road agent has turned out to be one himself!"

Drew said, "O'Doone, do you give your solemn oath that the man you saw with Fee's wagon was Tod Thorson?"

"I've already sworn that!"

"What was your wagon carrying?" Drew asked Fee.

"Whiskey and wallpaper."

"Was the cargo gone, O'Doone, when you found the wagon after Thorson had abandoned it?"

Rory hesitated, undecided as how to answer. "The whiskey was still there," he admitted.

"I had it fetched in this morning," Fee said.

"Then," said Drew, "you're accusing Thorson of risking his life on a wild ride down the mountain and dodging bullets in the bargain for the sake of stealing a few cases of *wallpaper?*"

"I don't know why he did it," Fee growled. "I only know that he did. When the *Trumpet* building caught fire last week, he accused me of setting that fire—even after I'd worked in the bucket brigade to put it out. He's got a grudge against me, it seems. Maybe he took my wagon as a step toward ruining

my freighting business, just to get even. I'm not interested in his motive. Road agenting is road agenting!"

Joe Coulter was possessed of a sudden inspira-
tion. "What are we wastin' time for?" he shrilled
from where he sat. "I tell you I creased that galoot!
Make him take off his shirt and show whether he's
wounded or not, the same as he wanted Rory to do
that time. Make him do it, I say!"

Lockhart had the stricken look of a man who sees
his cause go glimmering. Anguish in his eyes, he
glanced at Thorson. "Can you prove that you're not
wounded?" he asked.

"Of course not," Thorson said. "I've got a bandage over my ribs. I was shot yesterday."

"You admit that? By whose gun?"

And that was when the door burst open and
Ginny came into the hall, but only Thorson and Dr.
Drew knew that she had been lingering outside, perhaps for many minutes, and had been waiting for
just such a cue. She came down the aisle, a bundle
of papers still wet from the press over her arm, and
she passed them out to left and right as she walked
along. And because men sensed the dramatic in this
sudden entry of hers, they seized upon the papers
and those who didn't have one peered over the
shoulders of others, the cry, "What does it say?
What does it say?" going up.

"Thunder Gulch's first extra!" Ginny announced
and handed a paper to Zeke Lockhart. As he held it
up, those in the front rows could see the banner
headline which read: WHAT BECAME OF FEE'S
MISSING WALLPAPER?

"Read it out loud!" somebody shouted, and Lockhart nodded dazedly and began. " 'The citizens of
Thunder Gulch,' " he read, " 'are amusing themselves this afternoon at a trial to determine what
became of a cargo of wallpaper for Matthew Fee's

Hurdy-Gurdy House which somehow failed to arrive at its destination. The *Trumpet* is informed that J. Todhunter Thorson, marshal of Thunder Gulch, son of the town's founder, and part-time editor of this sheet, is accused of the theft. The *Trumpet* doesn't deny that Mr. Thorson might have an interest in a load of paper, since our own stock was destroyed in a fire of mysterious origin directly after Matthew Fee had been informed that the sheet intended to work against him. Mr. Thorson's interest in paper has since been increased by the loss, also under mysterious circumstances, of a new supply which was being freighted in. But we are not concerned about our own ill fortune. The pertinent questions still remains: what became of Matthew Fee's missing wallpaper . . . ?' "

"Look!" bawled a miner who had a copy of the *Trumpet*. "This newspaper is printed on wallpaper!"

"*My* wallpaper!" Fee cried.

"Why, yes, I believe it is," said Thorson. "With bluebirds. The symbol of happiness, Mr. Fee."

But he had a hard time making himself heard, for a great cry came from the crowd as men began to understand, and it was not the roar of fury but the roar of laughter that rose to the rafters and shook them. And in the midst of that thundering mirth, Matthew Fee made his hasty departure from the building, his men huddled behind him, and the echo of laughter was to follow them down the trail and into the gulch below.

Chapter Twelve
MADAM VIGILANTE

Tod Thorson had given Thunder Gulch a joke. To men who had almost forgotten how to laugh, men whose lives were a monotonous matter of toil and more toil, leavened only by such crude pleasures as were to be purchased in the camp, Thorson had brought laughter, a bit of humor of the lavish horse-play type they could understand. Thorson had needed paper for the *Trumpet*, its stock twice destroyed, and obviously by Matthew Fee. So Thorson had stolen Fee's wallpaper and printed the *Trumpet* upon it. More than that, he had allowed himself to be tried for the theft, pretended to be trying to squirm out of the charge, and then, with the trial going against him, he'd produced the missing wallpaper, thereby admitting the theft and outfoxing Matthew Fee.

It was a tale that was retold over many a bar that night, and it ran through the diggings like wildfire in the days that followed. Many a man was to sidle up to Thorson saying, "You ain't seen anything of Matt Fee's wallpaper, have you?", guffawing heartily as the question was put, slapping Thorson's back afterwards and insisting that he have a drink.

No issue of the *Thunder Gulch Trumpet* was ever scanned so intently as that one which was printed on the reverse side of a bluebird-patterned wallpaper. And there was more to be found in it than a source of merriment. The sheet contained an account of the organization of the vigilantes, an invitation was worded so that all who wished could understand, and the *Trumpet* office had a number of bearded, booted visitors that next week—men who asked questions, got answers, and went their way with a steadier stride.

He'd won the confidence of the miners, had Thorson, and when the vigilantes held a second meeting, this time in the great stone house of Lars Thorson, the strength of the organization was tripled when the oath in darkness was taken. Officers were elected; Dr. Huntley Drew was named president, and Tod Thorson and Zeke Lockhart were made executive officers, and there was much talk among the men about what might be done with this newfound strength of theirs.

"I know what is uppermost in the minds of all of you," Dr. Drew said. "You'd like to see your gold go out, and you'd like to be sure that it will go out safely. I echo your wish. Our own claim has been producing steadily, and we'd prefer to convert our gold into cash so that we might invest in better equipment. I assure you, gentlemen, that when the moment is ripe, we'll run the road agent gantlet. And if future meetings bring as many recruits to our organization, we'll soon be able to make a move."

But if the vigilantes were not yet ready to test their strength, the road agent legion was all too active. A man lay dead along the trail the very next dawn, a man who'd tried, even as Gaston Thiebault had tried, to sneak from the camp under cover of darkness. Josh Hoskins had his stagecoach stopped on the slant of the Wolverines; his passengers were stripped of all they carried, and one, putting valor above caution and trying for his gun, had his arm broken by a bullet. A miner who'd taken too much to drink was beset between the Hurdy-Gurdy House and his cabin, beaten and robbed. But it was the case of Eph Tutt that really stirred the diggings.

Eph, a garrulous graybeard with a weakness for telling tall and terrible stories, was found dead in his shack one gray dawn. The floorboard covering his hidden cache of dust was wrenched away, and the sign said that Eph Tutt had been tortured until he'd indicated that board.

And thus it went, violence begetting violence, until the laughter went out of Thunder Gulch, even its echo fading, and an evening came when Tod Thorson paced the big living room of Lars Thorson's house while Dr. Drew tried to preach him patience.

"We can only wait, Tod," Drew insisted. "If we tried going after the road agents, who could we arrest? Matthew Fee? Where's one scrap of real evidence to prove him a murderer? We're not a bunch of bloodletting renegades who can go hanging and shooting just because we've got suspicions. It would be better if we let the road agents run wild than if we hanged one innocent man. But sooner or later someone will overplay his hand, and we'll have a wedge to begin our prying."

"Rory O'Doone's showed himself in camp a couple of times lately," Thorson said. "That banishment decree still hangs over him, but the most I could do, as marshal, is run him out. That wouldn't cure the cancer that's eating at this camp. It's got to be hemp medicine from here on out—and an eye for an eye, and a tooth for a tooth. Drew, if a showdown doesn't shape up soon, we've got to force one!"

"Perhaps you're right," Drew said.

Thorson ceased his pacing. "Doctor, sometimes I think there's a spy among us! Oh, I know I shouldn't say that so long as I have nothing but suspicion. Yet the road agents seem to know every move that's made in camp. Look at Thiebault's case. It was common knowledge that he planned on leaving the diggings, but how did anybody know it would be so soon? Once I blamed the Kincaid woman for betraying him. Now I'm not so sure. And what about Eph Tutt who had the soles of his feet scorched till he told where his gold was hidden? Eph joined up

with us at the last meeting, and when there was talk
of sending the gold out, he admitted that he had a
bigger cache than was safe to keep around. Three
dozen men heard him say it. Have we played into
the road agents' hands by starting an organization
and sharing each other's secrets?"

Dr. Drew was sitting back beyond the wash of
light from the fireplace, and his voice came sooth-
ingly from the shadows. "Patience, boy, patience,"
he said. "If there's a spy—and I've wondered too—
we'll find him, just as we'll find every other man
who needs a hanging. Our day will come, and we'll
strike hard when it does."

Thorson strode to a window and had a look out at
the gulch, shapeless in the night, and as he looked,
he wondered what the next dawn would bring. "I
hope it's soon," he said. "I hope it's soon!"

Achilles had his heel and Rory O'Doone had his
whiskey, and the big road agent's fondness for a
bottle had mastered him this night. He had become
more daring, had Rory, appearing in camp whenever he pleased, and since no man challenged his
presence here, even Matthew Fee had lifted his ban,
no longer frowning upon the frequent appearances
of his lieutenant. Thus Rory, his pockets bulging
with dust, had been able to roister through the early
hours of the evening, dividing his time between the
dance floor of the Hurdy-Gurdy House and the bar,
spending his money for drinks and dance tickets
and monopolizing the attention of Belle Kincaid.

She had gotten into the blood of Rory O'Doone,
had Belle. To him, this woman who had lately come
to Thunder Gulch was from another world, a loftier
world than Rory had ever known, and he sensed the
breeding that was hers and hated it as something he
could never attain, his need to conquer her flaming
the higher because of his resentment. She had given

him no more than the mechanical smile of her adopted profession, and she'd danced with him only because the rules of the house forced her to do so. Or so Rory decided, and each drink increased the half-infatuation, half-hatred that had seized him. When she drew her cloak about her and left the building long before the last dance, he lurched outside after her, grasping at her elbow.

"Where you going?" he demanded thickly.

"To my cabin. I've got a headache, and I'm taking the rest of the night off."

"Gonna see you home," he insisted.

She might have used haughtiness as a weapon, and there'd been times when he'd quailed before it, but she knew it would be a feeble bulwark now. Studying him in the starlight, she kept her thoughts to herself, but her smile became warmer than it had ever been for him. "Of course," she said. "Thank you. The gulch is hardly a safe place to walk alone by night."

Astonished, Rory attempted a bow, and if she hadn't steadied him he'd have fallen on his face. She took his arm and they went along the street, the mountains looming awesome and tremendous around them, the inverted bowl of stars a shining canopy overhead, the night pressing thickly upon the camp. Rory mumbled incoherently as they walked along, and when they reached her cabin and she opened the door, he stumbled in after her, making no apology. She got a lamp aglow, and it lighted the single room with its bed and bureau and stove and scattering of chairs. Into one of these chairs lurched Rory, squinting approvingly about the cabin and bursting into song:

"I'll scrape the mountains clean, old girl,
    I'll drain the rivers dry.
I'm off for California, Susannah, don't you cry.

Oh, Susannah, don't you cry for me.
I'm off for California with my wash bowl
     on my knee-e . . ."

She said, "Sh-h-h! Someone will hear you! After
all, even a hurdy-gurdy girl has to keep one eye on
her reputation."

He laughed uproariously at that. "Used to be you
were too good for big Rory, eh? But you know who's
cock-of-the-walk in these diggings, don't you?" He
reached and drew her to him with coarse and meaning violence. "Come on, give us a kiss just to show
we're good friends now!"

She'd dealt with drunken men before, but she
knew that words and blandishments would mean
nothing to this one. There was a derringer in the
front of her dress, and that was good to remember.
Letting herself slip into his lap, she kissed him and
recognized the savage hunger of his lips for what it
was. She pulled herself away and began rummaging
in a dresser drawer. "I've whiskey here somewhere," she said quickly. "Let's have a drink together."

"Sure," Rory agreed. "To us! What the devil did a
woman like you want with an old coot like Pi Hazzard?"

She shrugged and laughed, but if he'd laid a hand
on her then he would have found her cold as the
wind that blew atop the Wolverines. "A girl gets
tired of living alone," she said. Then: "Who killed
him, Rory? Was it you?"

He waved a hand. "I dunno. Fee, maybe. Or one
of his boys. Hazzard was pretty small pumpkins."
He raised his voice again. "Oh, Sus-ann-ah, don't
you cry for me-e—"

She poured him a drink and he downed it and
reached for her again, but she eluded him by a

quick and apparently casual movement to put the bottle back on the bureau.

He said, "Sho you get tired of living alone, eh? How about you and me teaming up, Belle?"

"Me live with a miner?" She laughed. "To work and slave in a shack like this?"

He squinted one eye, drew a poke of gold dust from his pocket and carelessly tossed it to the floor. "A miner?" he scoffed thickly. "You shink—think Rory O'Doone spends hish time grubbing in the ground? Goldsh easier gotten than that!"

"Then you're a road agent," she said, her eyes growing big and wide. "Ah, but you're just bluffing!"

That stirred him to greater belligerency than she'd hoped for, and he said, "Bluffing, eh? You come and I'll show you shomethin'! Cabin in the canyon on the Old Shouth Road. Dozen men there, shavvy. Men that takes orders from Dory O'Roone—Rory O'Doone. Kingpinsh, thash's what I am!"

"Is it far away?"

He jerked at a rawhide thong across his shirt-front, produced a handsome gold watch, snapped it open and had a bleary-eyed look at it. "Can be there before midnight," he said. "Eashy."

She almost betrayed herself then, and it was the watch that did it. She'd seen it before, seen it in the possession of Gaston Thiebault that last night the little Canuck had been alive. Thus she knew that no part of what Rory O'Doone had confessed to-night had been mere braggadocio, and she also knew that she'd discovered as much from him as she'd ever need to know.

She said, "Another drink? But no, I think you've got far more now than you can handle."

That instantly made him belligerent again. "Not drunk!" he insisted and reached for the bottle. "Give it here!"

"Bet you a kiss you can't kill it." She smiled.

Tilting the bottle, he let the liquor run, and when he hurled the bottle into a corner it was empty. He reached for her, coming up out of the chair, and she barely managed to elude him, and she wondered if she were going to have to use the derringer after all. But his movement had sent him lurching against the bed; his feet gave away beneath him and he sprawled across the bed, lying there with arms outstretched. She watched, expecting to see him get up again, and then she became aware that he was snoring.

She tiptoed closer. He hadn't shaved for at least two days, his jaw was blue with stubble, his mouth hung open and the reek of him was sickening. For a moment she fought a weakening wave of nausea, and then, because there was much that had to be done—and quickly—she slipped her cloak about her shoulders, blew out the lamp and stepped from the cabin.

The darkness was the thicker for that brief hour in the lamplight, and she groped her way along, coming at last to the trail that climbed upward to the stone house Lars Thorson had built. The porch was a well of shadows, but she had conquered fears greater than any darkness could bring her, and she pounded upon the door resolutely and for a long time before it was opened.

Dr. Drew stood before her, a long white nightgown flapping about his ankles, a lamp in his hand. Tod Thorson was right behind him, but Thorson had taken time to draw on his trousers. She said impatiently, "Don't stand there with the light upon me, so that anybody can see! Let me in, please, and quickly!"

"I—I don't quite understand," Drew stammered.

Brushing past him into the hallway, she shoved the door shut behind her. Thorson said, "Let's go into the living room," and Drew led the way, setting the lamp upon a table. Belle said, "You two are heads of the new vigilante organization, aren't you?"

Drew held himself stiffly. "If you've come here to spy for Matthew Fee—" he began.

She made a nervous gesture with her hand. "We can't waste time sparring with words," she said. "I know all about your organization. So does Matthew Fee; I wormed the truth from him. There's nothing new you can tell me. You held your first meeting in Tom Conway's old mine, and I can name every man who was there. Does that convince you it isn't information I'm after?"

Thorson spoke up. "You see, Drew, there *is* a spy! I want to hear this woman out."

"Rory O'Doone is in my cabin, dead drunk and asleep," Belle said. "You can have him for the taking, and you'll find Frenchy Thiebault's watch on him. Don't you understand! He's one of the road agents. And tonight he told me that there's a road agent shebang in the canyon down the Old South Road. You can lay your hands on a bunch of them if you hurry!"

"If this is a trap—!" Drew began, but Thorson had grasped the truth quicker than he. Turning to Belle Kincaid, Thorson said, "Ma'am, it appears that I owe you an apology that can't be put into words. For the time, I'll just say I'm sorry and hope to prove it later. Doctor, don't you see! She's one of us! She's been one of us all along! And she's given us the very thing we need—a few road agents we can bag for a starter. Our hour has come—thanks to her!"

That took the last of the skepticism out of Drew, his eyes widening. "You're right, Tod!" he cried. "I believe you're right! Miss Kincaid, I owe you an apology too, but this isn't the time for it. Tod, we've got to get dressed and rouse every vigilante we can reach. We've done our waiting, and our waiting is over. We'll ride tonight, Tod, and we'll ride hard!''

Chapter Thirteen
HEMP MEDICINE

When Thorson and Dr. Drew came downstairs again, both of them dressed, Belle Kincaid was pacing the wide living room. Thorson said, "Doctor, if you don't mind, I'm going after O'Doone right away. No sense taking any chance of his slipping through our fingers. It's early enough that you'll likely find some of the vigilantes in the saloons. Once the word gets passed, it won't take long to gather enough to raid the South Road shebang."

Drew nodded his consent, and Thorson glanced at Belle. "You've done enough tonight to win either a medal or a bullet for yourself," Tod said. "Whether we've a traitor among us or not, I'd rather that no one guessed who'd acted as informer. That's another reason I'm going after Rory. I'd just as soon not have everybody know where and how we got hold of him."

From the look of her, he guessed that she was beyond fear, but she let him lead her to his own room on the second floor where she'd be out of sight when the vigilantes gathered. When Thorson left the house, Dr. Drew was already gone, and shortly a dozen men were to come to the stone house, and another dozen, all of them heavily armed, all solemn beneath the burden of a strange and terrifying responsibility. But Thorson did not witness that grim gathering, for he was gone about other business.

His boots crunching against the rocky trail, he was marching toward the Kincaid cabin when a voice hailed him. It was Zeke Lockhart, and with him was a lanky miner named Cory who'd been at that first meeting in Tom Conway's mine. The two were on their way from the camp to the diggings, and Lockhart said, "What brings you out so late, Tod?"

Thorson had come to respect and admire this gentle-eyed man, and he trusted Lockhart as he would have trusted a brother. He couldn't be so sure about Cory, but it wasn't the time for evasion. "Come along," he said. "I'll tell you what's up as we walk."

Thus as they approached the cabin, they were all three alert to a need for caution. Nearing the place, they fanned out, guns in hands, making their footsteps feathery till they drew their circle tight and stood before the cabin door. Thorson kicked it inward and put himself over the threshold with a sudden, sideways movement. Rory O'Doone still sprawled across the bed, snoring lustily.

They got the lamp alight, Lockhart lifted O'Doone's gun and his silver-inlaid bowie knife, and they shook the big road agent roughly, but it took several minutes of this kind of treatment before O'Doone opened his eyes, staring blearily about. Propping himself upon an elbow, he glared wildly. "What the hell—?" he said.

Thorson reached for the rawhide thong stretched across O'Doone's shirt, and when it broke loose, the watch was in his hand. "This was Gaston Thiebault's, Rory," he said. "It's evidence enough to hang you for his death. Get up on your feet and come along!"

But O'Doone still kept to the bed, sprawling there and staring at the three as though he were just beginning to see them. O'Doone was soberer than he'd been for many an hour, Thorson judged, for a measure of sanity was in the road agent's eyes, and a wild fear as well. He swallowed hard, his fingers faltering to his throat. *"Vigilantes!"* he said.

Coming off the bed, he stood with his hands out

before him as though he might, in this manner, ward off the doom that had closed in upon him. He said, "You ain't gonna hang me, boys? You ain't thinkin' of that? All you've got to do is banish me from the gulch! Give me an hour and you'll never see me again!"

Zeke Lockhart showed his acute disgust. "Banish you?" he said. "We did that once, and you came back to spill a good man's blood along the trail. It's the rope this time, Rory. You can't talk yourself out of it. Hemp medicine is the cure for your breed, and you're getting the first dose!"

O'Doone looked from one unyielding face to another, ran his tongue along his lips, looked toward the door and saw that it was beyond his reach, and what happened then was not what Thorson had expected. For suddenly O'Doone's knees gave beneath him, and he went to the floor, flinging his arms around Thorson's legs. "Not the rope!" O'Doone babbled, a man without pride or hope. "Not the rope, Thorson! Put a bullet or a knife into me, but don't hang me! I don't want to die that way! Please, Thorson! I ain't any more guilty than the rest. Four of us did for Frenchy. Let me go and I'll tell you who they are and where you can lay your hands on them!"

Lockhart and Cory knelt to break O'Doone's grip and drag him from Thorson. Feeling sick to his stomach, Tod turned away, for he had looked at Rory O'Doone's soul and seen what a weak and spiritless thing it was, and the sight had not been good. He said, "And I'll bet Frenchy died fighting!"

"It wasn't me killed him!" Rory cried. "Buck Doheny had the shotgun. I won the watch from Buck in a poker game. Lewiston Pete Lucas was in on that deal, and so was Harry Pease. I wasn't the only one! I'm coming clean, boys! Can't you savvy that?"

Thorson looked away. "Take him to the stone

house," he said. "We'll have to give him a trial. And there's other work to be done tonight."

They had to half-carry Rory O'Doone; his feet refused to support him, and he muttered and moaned in his fear as they dragged him along, begging, pleading, and trying halfhearted threats. To all this the three turned stony ears, and when they reached Lars Thorson's house, O'Doone was bound hand and foot and thrust into that storeroom off the lower hallway where once he'd forced entry to rummage through Dr. Drew's luggage. Cory was left to guard the prisoner, and Thorson and Lockhart went to the living room where they found Dr. Drew and a few vigilantes.

Thorson made his report, and Dr. Drew said, "Doheny, Lucas and Pease, eh? That gives us some names for a starter. I'm not surprised that O'Doone crumbled. The loudmouthed, bragging kind usually does when the pressure comes. A few minutes ago I sent Pat Shea and a bunch of men down to the Old South Road. Likely they'll bag Doheny and the others at the cabin. At least we'll avenge Thiebault tonight."

"I'd like to be in on that South Road raid," Thorson said. "Maybe if I hurry I can catch up with Shea."

But before he left the house, he climbed the stairs to his room. Belle Kincaid was still here, and Ginny was with her. The girl had drawn a robe over her nightgown, and she sat on the edge of the bed beside the older woman. "Father asked me to come and stay with her," Ginny explained. "I couldn't sleep with a score of men tramping about the house."

"Rory O'Doone has been arrested," Thorson said to Belle. "It might be better if you went back to your cabin now. If somebody should be curious as to where you are tonight, they'd expect to find you there."

She caught his point; he could see that. She said, "Very well," and he wondered what it would take to put life in her voice and light in her eyes. Escorting her down the stairs and into the darkness of the porch, he took off his sombrero and cradled it under his arm. "You'll be safe, I'm sure," he said. "If I wasn't sure, I'd keep you here. But the only one who might guess the truth is Rory himself, and he'll be dead before sunup. Good night, Belle. I'm thanking you—for Thunder Gulch."

He found her hand and lifted it to his lips, and she said in a queer voice, "But it won't bring him back to life, will it?"

He had no answer for that, so he watched her walk away, and then he went to the grouped saddle-horses which the vigilantes who were inside had left tied to the porch railing. Helping himself to one of these mounts, he stepped into the saddle and turned toward the east when he reached the bottom of the slope. Clattering down the night-swathed street, he saw the light spilling from the Hurdy-Gurdy House and heard the beat of music, and he thought of Matthew Fee and wondered when the man would discover what was happening tonight. But Matthew Fee would keep, so Thorson galloped on across the barren flat to where the road forked. He turned to the south then, hurrying along, and soon he saw better than a dozen horsemen looming ahead of him. Starlight gleamed dully on a revolver barrel and one who rode to the rear said, "Who are you, mister?"

"Thorson," he replied and moved on up to where Pat Shea rode. "We've got Rory O'Doone," Thorson told him. "He's named Buck Doheny, Pete Lucas and Harry Pease as the bunch who were with him when Thiebault was murdered. I'm hoping we'll find them ahead."

Shea took the news with a grunt and they rode

onward, coming between the steep walls of the canyon until they were well past the place where Thorson had abandoned Matthew Fee's wagon. And then a rider said, "I remember the cabin. An old prospector used it till he died. We're not more than a quarter of a mile from it."

That brought them all down out of their saddles, and they held a short and low-voiced council before spreading out on foot, making a long, thin semicircle of men as they moved onward until the cabin loomed before them. The structure bulked darkly, no wisp of smoke showing from its chimney, but a half-dozen saddlers stomped in the corral beneath the canyon wall, one horse neighing loudly as they approached. Thorson was among those who faced the door, and he abandoned caution then, charging forward and kicking open the door and using that same sideways motion that had put him into Belle Kincaid's cabin.

This one was single-roomed too, but the room was larger and had built-in bunks against three of its walls, an indication that the road agents had remodeled this place for their own use. Others were crowding in behind Thorson, hurrying to the bunks with their guns ready. There was a great deal of startled cursing as men were wrenched from sleep, hauled to their feet and herded outside, and thus six prisoners were lined up.

"Some of our birds have flown," Thorson observed. "Rory said there'd be a dozen here."

A vigilante nodded toward a bucktoothed man with a yellowish cast to his skin. "That's Buck Doheny," he said. "The hairy little fellow with the big nose is Lewiston Pete, and the one who looks like a preacher is Harry Pease. We've collected that much hemp fodder at least."

Scowling, Buck Doheny said, "Just what the devil do you jiggers think you're doing?" But nobody made him answer, the corralled horses were silently saddled, the six hoisted to the hulls and lashed there. Shea said, "Touch a match to that shebang, somebody." Then the cavalcade was formed and began wending back to Thunder Gulch.

Midnight was past when they came along the street, the Hurdy-Gurdy House was closing for the night, and one of its employees stood in the doorway, gaping at the passing mounted men. The fellow quickly turned, vanishing into the building, and Thorson saw that startled movement. But he said nothing to Shea or the others as they rode on to the stone house. Here the prisoners were unloaded and hurried into the storeroom where Rory O'Doone still sprawled under the watchful eye of Cory. Doheny looked at the scar-faced road agent, spat and said, "Lucky at cards, eh? Now I'm beginning to understand!"

Thorson eyed Cory. "Need more guards?"

Cory shook his head, the vigilantes trooped into the living room to join the others, making a full two dozen and more, as many as could be found on short notice. Shea reported the South Road raid, and when he'd finished there was a tight, singing silence, for all the work was finished save for one last chore. Dr. Drew cleared his throat. "We'll have to hold trial," he said. "All the charter vigilantes are here except Quong Lee and Josh Hoskins. Word was sent to them, but it doesn't look like they'll be coming, so we might as well get on with the business. Let's bring in those three who weren't named in connection with the Thiebault killing. The longer the others have to wait, the more anxious they'll be to talk when their time comes."

Thus three of the prisoners were soon herded into the big room, their feet unbound but their hands still tied behind them. Blinking in the lamplight, one said, "What in blazes do you figger you can do with us?"

Drew glanced at his fellow vigilantes. "Anybody know these men?"

"Charlie Wagner's the tall one. The other two are the Strunk brothers, Zack and Thad."

"You three were captured at a road agent she-bang," Drew said sternly. "You were found in the company of men whom we know to be murderers. If you're not of the same breed, then what were you doing there?"

Wagner shrugged defiantly. "We were prospectin' up the canyon," he declared. "We saw a light in the cabin, found those other three jiggers there and asked 'em if we could use the bunks. Can you prove it different, vigilante?"

That put Drew in a quandary, and he looked to the massed vigilantes. "Anybody know of these men ever being mixed up in road agent business?" he asked.

It took a while for anybody to make an answer. "They hang around Fee's place a lot," Lockhart finally spoke up. "We've all had notions about them. That's all."

Thorson said, "Doctor, you mentioned earlier to-night that it would be better to let the road agents run wild than to hang one innocent man. I'd say we haven't got hanging evidence against these three. But let's move them to one of the upstairs rooms and hold them till after the trials are over. That will leave those other four worried as to what actually happened. Then bring in Doheny, Lucas and Pease, leaving O'Doone to sweat some more. I've got a reason, Drew. I'll tell you about it later."

Drew gave him a long and thoughtful look, then shrugged. "Shea," he said. "Take these fellows up-stairs and keep them under your gun. And someone fetch the other three from the storeroom."

"I will," Thorson volunteered.

He came down the hallway to the little anteroom. "Take Lucas and those other two in to the vigilantes, Cory," he said. "Then come back to keep an eye on O'Doone. I'll watch him while you're gone."

Cory nodded, and when he'd herded the three up the hallway, Thorson was alone with O'Doone. He looked at the big road agent for a long time, saying nothing, the silence running until it was beyond the endurance of Rory O'Doone. "What about Charlie Wagner and the Strunk boys?" the road agent demanded. "Have you taken them to stretch rope? Tell me, Thorson! Come on, man! There's no harm in telling me!"

But still Thorson held silent, seeing the glistening sweat on O'Doone's face and the stark fear in his eyes and gauging these signs for what they might be worth. Then: "Who killed Pi Hazzard, O'Doone? I can't promise you anything for the answer, and we can only hang you once, and we'll be doing that for Thiebault's death. But I'd like to know about Hazzard. Did you get him, Rory? Or did Fee? His office window looks down on the spot where Hazzard fell."

"Then he done it!" O'Doone cried shrilly. "He must have. I was down at the bar, doing some drinking, when it happened. I can prove it, Thorson! Matt Fee's the road agent boss. I'm only one of his boys. Fee's the one you want! Ask him about Hazzard—and about Eph Tutt and a lot of others! He's got a hundred hangings coming to him!"

Thorson's pulse quickened, for this was much more than he'd hoped to learn, and he turned toward the door as he heard Cory's footsteps. But the frantic babbling of O'Doone was like a hand upon his shoulder, restraining him. "Drew's the head man of the vigilantes, isn't he? Send him here,

Thorson! Tell him I want to talk to him alone! I'll tell him everything!''

But Thorson made no promise, and when he came back to the big room he saw Doheny and Lucas and Pease standing sullenly before Dr. Drew and there was something in the very air to tell Thorson that the trial was over. Drew said, ''We faced them with the evidence, Doheny cursed us out, but he's admitted the truth. We were about to take a vote. Since you didn't hear the trial, Tod, we'll vote without you.''

Then: ''All those who consider these men guilty of murder, step over by the fireplace.''

They were slow getting started, those vigilantes. But Thorson could see that that was not because they had their doubts, but was because they were men with no liking for the choice they had to make. One of them began the movement and another followed, and then they were all crowded over by the fireplace. Buck Doheny broke into a steady, monotonous cursing, Lewiston Pete stood stonyfaced and Harry Pease began to sob. Dr. Drew wilted into a chair, passed his hand across his forehead and kept his eyes away from the three.

''Take them out and hang them,'' he said.

Again the vigilantes were hesitant, but they came and laid hands upon the three, moving toward the doorway with them. Thorson waited until they were gone, then stepped toward Dr. Drew. ''I've talked to O'Doone,'' Tod said. ''He told me that Fee was the one who killed Hazzard. Maybe he's lying in the hopes of saving his own neck; I don't know. He wants to talk to you—alone. He's scared out of his skin, and I think he'll tell you everything we need to know.''

''I'll go see him,'' Drew said.

''And I'm going to arrest Matthew Fee. O'Doone's told me enough to give me the right to do that.''

"You're not going alone, Tod!"

Thorson smiled without humor. "Is Fee that wide across the britches?"

Drew said, "I think I know what's on your mind, Tod. It may be foolish, but go and have your fling at it. And good luck."

"Thanks," Thorson said and went out of the house. Coming down the trail into the gulch, he saw the group ahead of him, the group that had come to a halt beneath a gnarled old cottonwood whose outspread branches traced a weird pattern against the night sky. He knew what that group was about to do, and even though he had a need for haste, he paused here, held as a man is held in a nightmare, powerless to move, powerless to drag his eyes from the stark and somber scene he witnessed. It wasn't pretty, and it wasn't to his liking, but he would remember it to the last of his days.

"Got those nooses built?" Zeke Lockhart was asking, he of the gentle voice and the gentle ways, his words drifting low and ghostly. And that slithering sound was a rope scraping over a low limb of the tree, and there was another such sound, and another, until three dangling nooses were silhouetted. Harry Pease's voice rose, sobbing. "I don't want to die! I don't want to die! *I ain't fit to die!*" Lewiston Pete Lucas was silent, Buck Doheny was laughing boisterously, but the sound had a hysterical edge to it. Now the three were up on horses and under the ropes, and Doheny was saying, loud and distinctly, "See you all in hell, boys! Here goes nothin'!" A vigilante was praying, another was cursing. Explosive slaps were sending the three horses bolting, and three forms writhed beneath the cottonwood. Somebody said, "That makes it even, Frenchy. That makes it even!"

All this Tod Thorson saw and heard before he dragged his eyes away and put his back to the scene.

But in his mind's eye, he could still see those three men dancing upon air, and the picture was both frightful and satisfying, made as it was from a grim and revolting need that honest men could no longer deny.

Thus, at long last, the law had come to Thunder Gulch.

Chapter Fourteen
THE FIGHT AT FEE'S PLACE

Matthew Fee had his ornate office to himself this night. He was wedged into one of the plush-covered chairs, his feet crossed on the desk before him, when he heard the music fade to a finish. His trips to the scrolled sideboard had been frequent enough that drink had given a high flush to his florid face and filled him with a mellow contentment, and he lazily marked the time by the banjo clock on the wall and knew that another closing hour had come to his Hurdy-Gurdy House.

Now he heard the swift movement of feet down the hallway; the door opened and one of his housemen stood at the threshold. The fellow's name was Jake DeSpain, and he was tall and flat-chested and had been dying of a lung ailment for quite a long time. A green eye-shade gave his cadaverous face a weird and ghastly hue, and Fee frowned at the sight of him, his first thought being that Jake DeSpain had come to bring the night's take to the office. But there hadn't been time for the gold dust to have been gathered, so Fee said petulantly, "What the devil is it, man?"

DeSpain said, "I just saw better than twenty horsemen heading along the gulch toward the west. It was Thorson and a bunch of his friends. But six of those riders were roped to their saddles—the Strunk boys, Buck Doheny, Lewiston Pete, Charlie Wagner and Harry Pease. I come fast to tell you, boss."

Something in the harried look of DeSpain was oddly irritating to Fee. He took his feet down off the desk and said, with a great show of assurance, "So the vigilantes have finally made a move. I wondered when they would." Moving out of his chair, he took to pacing the room, making many restless crossings then moving toward a chair where he'd tossed his coat and gun-belt. But he stopped in midstride. "No, it might be better if I didn't show myself," he said. "Jake, go out and see what you can see. Come back and report as soon as you can. Go ahead, man! They've nothing on you except the fact that you work for me!"

DeSpain went out, closing the door behind him, and Fee moved toward it, touching the key. But he changed his mind and did not lock it. Stepping to the sideboard, he had a hasty drink, part of it dribbling down his shirtfront, and he began his pacing again, pausing at the window frequently and staring down into the dark tunnel of the street. When he judged that DeSpain had been gone better than a half hour, the last of his patience ran out; but still there was nothing to do but wait. And finally DeSpain returned.

He came into the office hastily, his eyes holding the look of one who has seen the worst of his fears realized, and he said jerkily, "They've hanged Doheny, Lucas and Pease, hanged them to that big cottonwood just below Lars Thorson's house. When I first come, there was saddlers strung out all around Thorson's place, and lights blazing in the windows. After a while they dragged those three out and to the tree. My God, Fee, do you see what it means?"

Fee could see all too clearly, but he kept a tight hold and his fear did not run away with him. Putting his hand on DeSpain's stooped shoulder, he said, "What about the others, man? What about the Strunks and Charlie Wagner?"

"They were talking about them, after the hanging. Some of the vigilantes were for hanging the Strunks and Charlie, too. Zeke Lockhart made a speech

about a fair trial and them not having evidence
enough to string up the others. But I wouldn't give a
plugged peso to be in their boots."

Fee turned this over in his mind and found a core
of consolation in DeSpain's story. "They're doing
business in a law-abiding fashion," Fee mused
aloud. "That means that most of the boys are safe
enough, unless they let their foot slip." He let go of
DeSpain and turned to pace. "Jake, you and the
boys will have to run the house for a while," he
decided. "I've got to clear out till I can find a way to
break the back of this vigilante outfit. You can see
that. I'll hide out at the Michigan Hole shebang for a
while. Pass the word to all the boys to meet me
there. Have you got that straight?"

DeSpain nodded with no great enthusiasm, and
Fee measured the man with a long and intent look.
"Jake," he said, "the vigilantes have gold, and they
may try buying evidence. They might even make a
dicker with you. You know what would happen to
any man who double-crossed me, Jake."

DeSpain swallowed hard. "I reckon I do."

"Get on about your business," Fee ordered. "And
get that worried look off your face. This game isn't
over, by a long shot. And when it's finished, you'll
still find Matthew Fee the gent worth the backing."

He shoved DeSpain outside and closed the door
after him, but once Fee was alone again, his movements were quick and precise. Fetching a handsome
leather valise out of a corner closet, he went to a
safe built into the wall, spun its dial and swung back
the ponderous door. Most of his gold had gone out
of the gulch and had been turned into currency and
securities, so there were many packages to be
stowed into the valise, and a few pokes of dust as
well. The valise full to bulging, he strapped it shut
and stepped toward his coat and gun-belt, across
the room. The door opened then, the sound jerking

him, and he said, "What the devil is it now, Jake?"
But when he turned to look, it wasn't Jake who
stood in the doorway.

Fee made a wild and desperate lunge for the gun-
belt then, but Tod Thorson said, "You'll never reach
it, Fee. Not alive. Stand your hand, mister. You're
under arrest!"

When Thorson had put his back to the hangtree
and come down to the strewn planks of the camp,
he'd seen a figure scurry past him and ahead, and
he recognized the fellow as one of Fee's housemen.
Whether it was the one who had witnessed the vigilante entry into town a short while before, he
couldn't be sure. But when the man hurried into the
Hurdy-Gurdy House, Thorson loitered in the shadows, studying the lighted window of Fee's office
above and doing a great deal of debating as to
whether he should venture into Fee's place alone.

It wasn't fear that held him, but the thought of a
necessity greater than his own. The vigilantes
wanted Matthew Fee, kingpin of the road agents.
The sight of that houseman, hurrying to his master,
was evidence enough that Fee was at this very moment being informed of the turn events had taken.
Fee, therefore, would be prepared for trouble, and
Thorson knew he should take no chance that might
mean Fee's slipping beyond the vigilantes' reach.
Yet it was a personal grudge that had brought Thorson here alone, a grudge Dr. Drew had been quick
to understand. Fee had once hurled a challenge at
Thorson, and Tod had not forgotten. Tonight might
be the last chance to accept that challenge, yet doing so might jeopardize the vigilante cause.

All these things Thorson turned over in his mind
as he waited, and then he realized that to go and
fetch the vigilantes now would be to give Fee the
very opportunity to escape that the man might be
wanting. Shrugging, he strode to the door of the

Hurdy-Gurdy House. Jake DeSpain was just preparing to bolt that door, but Thorson put his shoulder against it and shoved inside. The huge room seemed larger in its emptiness, the musicians were long gone from the raised platform, and only DeSpain was around. To him Thorson said, "I want to see Matthew Fee."

"He's not here," DeSpain answered hastily.

"Then he's wasting good coal-oil, burning a lamp in an empty office," Thorson said and stepped past DeSpain.

Out of the corner of his eye, he saw the houseman make a quick movement, and he spun, his fingers clamping on DeSpain's right wrist. Jerking a tiny derringer from the man's pocket, Thorson sent the gun clattering across the floor, then shoved DeSpain violently. "Don't try anything like that again!" Thorson said. "And don't raise a holler!"

Crossing the room, he skirted the gambling wing and climbed the stairs to the dark hallway. He threaded it to Fee's door, stepped inside and heard the man say, "What the devil is it now, Jake?" When Fee turned and saw him, Thorson took a second to enjoy the man's astonishment, then reached for his gun, clipping off the challenge that stopped Fee in midstride.

"So I'm under arrest," Fee sneered. "It's your hand, Thorson. A gun makes a big man out of a little one."

Thorson crossed over to Fee's gun-belt, lifted it and sent it sailing into a corner. Then he backed to the door, twisted the key and unlatched his own gun-belt. "I was hoping you'd say something like that, Fee," he said as his belt clattered to the floor and his gun fell after it. "It's all I needed to make me handle this my own way. Are you ready to try what you were going to do the night of the *Trumpet* fire?"

Visibly astonished, Fee said, "You don't mean—?"

"I could slap your face with a glove, the old-fashioned way," Thorson said. "Is that what it will take to start you?"

Fee understood him then. Thorson could see it in his eyes, and he could see a measure of assurance return to the man as Fee came at him with a throaty bellow, all arms and flailing fists. It was a wild rush, and there was the width of the room to give it impetus, but Thorson stepped wide and put the power of his right arm behind his bunched knuckles as he slammed them into Fee, just above the belt line. That staggered the big man, bringing a grunt from him, and he turned, wrapping his arms around Thorson. The two of them went lurching across the room like that, tangled together and straining against each other.

This was not as Thorson had planned to fight. He couldn't match Fee's power or bulk, and in a contest where only those things counted, the big man would quickly wear away the wiry edge of Thorson's strength. That night in the *Trumpet* building, he'd felt the ponderous weight of Fee. Tonight he'd hoped to outpoint Fee, to win by quick footwork and quick thinking. But there was no using these things now, not with Fee holding him in a close hug. They brought up hard against the desk and went over it, and as they crashed to the floor, Fee's grip was broken. Thorson rolled away, gaining enough distance to get to his feet.

Turning, he met Fee with a barrage of blows, planting them with planned precision and dancing out of Fee's way. The big man's look of surety gave way to something made of fear and disbelief, and to Thorson that, in itself, was half a victory. Pressing harder, he hammered at the face and body of Fee until he had the man wheezing and uncertain of movement.

But Fee had a lot of pounds to him, and murder was behind the might of his arms. Such of his blows as took toll had Thorson's head ringing, filling him with a great and numbing weariness. Fee had been schooled in the rough-and-tumble fighting of the frontier; he had no understanding of this will-o'-the-wisp art of Thorson's, and he tried desperately to get Thorson into the circle of his arms again.

Once Fee almost succeeded. A blow not dodged in time brought Thorson down on one knee, and Fee cried, "Now, damn it!" and came straight at him. But Thorson lunged up off the floor, butting his head into the pit of Fee's stomach. The man fell back with a gasping sob, and Thorson pressed his advantage with a flurry of fists. Dissipation was counting against Fee, his wind was all but gone, but it was still anybody's fight, and Thorson's driving thought was to finish it quickly. And then his chance came.

Their struggle had taken them to every part of the room; now they came edging toward the door. Thorson's gun-belt lay close by, forgotten in the fight. But Fee had spied it, his eyes betraying him as he stooped to grasp at the weapon, and Thorson anticipated his intent. More than that, he saw Fee's jaw exposed as it had never been before, so Thorson put the last of his strength behind his fist as he let go. Fee went down beneath that blow, collapsing in a stunned and bloody heap, and Thorson stood over him for a moment, heaving and panting. Then his own legs turned useless, and he fell heavily across Matthew Fee.

But consciousness hadn't completely deserted Thorson. He lay gasping, sucking in air with an effort, but he managed to get to his feet before Fee stirred. Dragging his gun and belt from beneath Fee, he latched the belt about his middle and staggered over to the sideboard. Selecting the largest bottle he could find, he emptied it into Fee's face.

The man blinking up at him, Thorson put his hand to Fee's collar and jerked him to his feet. "You're still under arrest," Tod said. "What's left of you belongs to the vigilantes."

Fee put his hand to his jaw. "What's your evidence against me?"

"O'Doone talked, Fee. I wouldn't tell you that, only O'Doone is likely dead by now and beyond anything you might ever get the chance to do about it. Get into your coat and get moving!"

He had a look into Fee's valise and hoisted it to fetch along. Most of the money had probably been stolen, and there might be ways to make restitution. Unlocking the door, he shoved Fee into the hallway and prodded the man ahead of him down the stairs. Jake DeSpain still lingered in the big dance room, but he made no move, staring sullenly as Thorson, crossing with his prisoner, left the building.

The stars had faded; another hour or so and this long night would be finished. Thorson put his hand on Fee's shoulder and headed the man along the gulch, and Thorson's gun, holstered and left hanging, was the symbol of his triumph. There was blood on his shirt, he discovered, and he couldn't understand that until he realized that the bandage over his ribs had slipped during the fight, and his gunshot wound, nearly healed, had broken open. The two of them came at last to the huge cottonwood and Thorson, peering, saw only three men hanging where he'd expected there'd be four by this time.

He couldn't understand that, but he'd get his answer in the lighted stone house up the slope.

Coming to the hall, the storeroom was dark and empty as he passed it, and he found the vigilantes massed in the big room, Dr. Drew in their midst, sunk in a chair, his beard in wild disarray, his collar open at the throat. Thorson would have asked about that at once, but there was a startled murmur as he shoved Matthew Fee into the room and let the valise thud to the floor. "Here he is, boys," he said. His battered face, and Fee's, told half the story, but he made no explanation.

Drew stirred. "One of you boys take Fee upstairs," he said.

A pair of men moved, grasping Fee by the arms and leading him from the room. Drew said, "I told these men that you'd gone after Fee. We talked it over meanwhile and decided we'll try him later. And we'll hang him in different fashion than we hanged those others. We've made a fine start tonight, Tod, and we'll show our hand from here on out. Fee will be given a public trial and a public hanging. It will be a deal calculated to prove to every decent man in these diggings that real law has come to stay. We've released Wagner and the Strunks. We haven't hanging evidence against them and, free, they'll carry word that will have every road agent jumping at his own shadow."

"And O'Doone?" Thorson asked. "You've got him upstairs? You're holding him for public trial?"

"O'Doone escaped," Drew said.

"Escaped!"

"His sending for me was a trick, Tod. He'd managed to get his hands untied somehow, but he fooled Cory by keeping his hands behind him. When I went to him alone, he did a lot of foolish babbling that sounded like he might be ready to make a complete confession naming every road agent in the camp. Then he asked me to come closer so he could whisper names to me. I did, and he got his hands on my throat and choked the senses out of me. The others found me when they came into the house after hanging those three. O'Doone went out through the window, it appears. Some of the boys are looking for him."

Thorson took that news as he might have taken a

blow, but when he looked at Drew and saw the bitterness in the man's scholarly face, he lifted his shoulders in a shrug. "One man's escape doesn't mean much, Drew," he said. "Either we'll bag Rory, or we'll never see him in this camp again. As I see it, we've all done a good night's work."

Chapter Fifteen
DREW'S DIARY

The vigilantes were gone, the great house of Lars Thorson lay silent, and only Dr. Drew and Tod Thorson stood before the fireplace. Tod had put his bandage back in place and tended to his bruises, and now the lamp had burned low, the fire turned to embers. At long last Dr. Drew spoke. "Time we were getting to bed, Tod," he said. "But before we part, I want to thank you for overlooking my mistake—the only mistake anyone made tonight. I'm sorry about Rory O'Doone."

"He doesn't matter so much," Thorson said and wished that that were true. "But I'm worried about Matthew Fee. Perhaps we should stand guard."

"It won't be necessary. It's a long drop to rocky ground from the window of that front bedroom. And I had our men remove the bedding and anything else Fee might think to use to build a rope. Also, the door lock is solid. Fee will be safe till we're ready to move him. And we'll move him only once."

"Then our work's about finished," Thorson said. "Your leadership did it, Drew—that and the courage of Belle Kincaid. Once Matthew Fee is finished, I think we'll find every road agent gone from the diggings. Rory O'Doone isn't the man to hold them together. He proved that, the day of the election."

"I suppose that's true," Drew mused. "Already the vigilantes are talking about moving their gold over the trail to Benton. You heard them as we broke up tonight. And once Fee is hanged, I think we'll be able to organize our treasure train. You have heartened me, Tod. Perhaps tonight was all to the good after all."

He lifted the lamp from the table, Thorson following after him as they went up the stairs to their rooms. Thorson bade Drew good night at the doctor's doorway, then strode on to his own room where he found the door ajar and a lamp burning dimly on the dresser. When he closed the door behind him, Ginny rose from the edge of his bed, lifting her finger to her lips for silence.

"Ginny!" he said.

She'd been here when Belle Kincaid had hidden in this room, but he'd supposed that Ginny was long since fast asleep in her own room. But she was as he'd last seen her, a robe pulled over her nightgown, her hair let down to her shoulders, and the lamplight had tangled in her tresses, giving them a shimmering radiance. She'd have made an appealing picture if it hadn't been for the fear in her eyes. He opened his arms as she came toward him, and he held her close, saying, "What is it, Ginny?"

"I've waited for you ever so long," she said, and her voice told him she'd been crying. "I've got to tell you about it, Tod. Father deliberately *let* Rory O'Doone escape!"

He wanted to say, "I don't believe it!" but his throat went dry. "Tell me about it," he finally managed.

"I went back to my own room after Miss Kincaid left," she said. "I tried to go to sleep, but I couldn't. There was too much excitement in the air—men tramping about, voices rumbling down below. And then everything became quiet—very quiet . . ."

"That was when our men took Doheny and Lucas and Pease outside," Thorson said.

"I went downstairs," Ginny went on. "I had to know what was going on. And as I came along the hall, I recognized voices in the storeroom—father's and Rory O'Doone's. Father was saying, 'There's one thing you seem to have forgotten, O'Doone. I can have you hanging before you get a chance to speak. The club you hold over me won't do you much good when you're dead.' Or some such words as that."

"And O'Doone said—?"

" 'You ain't getting out that easy, Doc. The night the girl caught me going through your trunk, I found out just about all I needed to know. And what I found out is written down on a piece of paper. A friend of mine has it, and he'll know what to do with it if I die. Now are you going to let me out of this? You can claim my hands were untied all the time. I'll rough you up a little to make it look good.' "

"And your father agreed?"

"He came to the door then. He looked up and down the hall, probably to make sure that nobody was around. And he saw me!"

Thorson whistled softly.

"He came and grabbed me by the shoulders," Ginny said. "I'd never seen him look as he did then. 'How long have you been standing here?' he said. 'What have you heard?' I said, 'Nothing! I just came down to see why everything was so quiet.' He kept hold of me for nearly a minute, and then he said, 'Go to your room, Virginia! Go to your room at once and go to bed!' I was scared stiff. I came up to my room, and after a while a couple of vigilantes came upstairs to release those three men they'd locked in the front bedroom. One said, 'We had seven to start with. Rory escapes, and now we turn these three loose and hand them their guns and horses! We'd do better if we used a rope on them!' Then I knew that father *had* let Rory escape, and I came to your room to wait and tell you about it. Oh, Tod, what does it mean? What is the club that Rory holds over him that made him do a thing like that?"

Thorson said, "I don't know. And I won't believe

he really betrayed us till I have all the truth. You're
not forgetting that he's your father, Ginny?''

"Do you think that telling on him was easy for
me?" she asked. "But I had to do it, Tod. I didn't
take the oath in darkness. That wasn't for women.
But I couldn't be less of a vigilante than Belle Kincaid. The dream of Lars Thorson and Pi Hazzard
means something to me, too.''

After a long moment of silent thought, he kissed
her gently. "Go to bed now, dear," he said. "And
don't worry about this. I'll take care of everything. I
promise you that.''

His arm about her trembling shoulders, he took
her up the hallway to her own room. He'd left his
door open, and lamplight spilled out into the hall
and touched the trunk of Dr. Drew, shoved up
against the wall. Drew had had his luggage removed
from the storeroom downstairs right after O'Doone
had gone through it, but the trunk had been put
here in the hall till such times as Drew made room
for it inside. Coming back along the hall, Thorson
studied the trunk thoughtfully, crossed to Drew's
door and put his ear to it. Drew was breathing
evenly, apparently asleep. Unhesitantly Thorson
opened the trunk and delved into its littered con-
tents.

He found the leather-bound book which Ginny
had once wrenched away from O'Doone, and he
also found a large envelope marked IMPORTANT.
Taking these two articles into his room, he looked
into the envelope first. It held papers, some old,
some new, a certificate of membership in an honor-
ary archeological society, a few letters from Jamieson Hazzard to Drew, a marriage certificate and a
birth certificate.

The marriage certificate had been issued to Huntley Wadsworth Drew and Louis Elizabeth Wish in
St. Louis more than twenty years ago. Thorson pon-

dered over the woman's name for a long moment
before it came to him, very abruptly, that Wish,
the maiden name of Ginny's mother, also belonged
to Dr. Absalom Wish, longtime associate of Dr.
Drew's.

The birth certificate was Ginny's, and was dated
some two years after the marriage of Drew and Louise Wish. Thorson looked it over, thrust the papers
into the envelope and was about to set the envelope
aside when he noticed the names hand-printed on
the back of it. They had been put there recently, he
judged; the ink hadn't faded, and they were
scrawled in the absent fashion of a man who has let
his thoughts run away with him while holding a pen
in his hand. Lars Thorson's name was there, and
Jamieson Hazzard's and—this lifted Thorson's
brows—Quong Lee's and Rory O'Doone's. The first
three names had lines drawn through them, and after O'Doone's there was a series of question marks.

Upon all this Thorson put a puzzled speculation,
and with no answer forthcoming, he turned to
Drew's diary. This was the book which Drew had
claimed was valueless to anybody but himself, the
account of his last expedition with Dr. Wish.
Thumbing the pages, Thorson found a dry and de-
tailed description of the fitting out of that expedition, its arrival at a Mexican port, and of the long
journey into the jungles at the Yucatán-Guatemala
border. He'd about decided that this hadn't been the
source of whatever information Rory O'Doone possessed, when he found this entry:

> The excavations of Chichen Itzá are behind us,
> and with the capital of the Ancient Mayan Empire
> a day to the rear, I'm wondering when we'll see
> the face of another white man. Ab cannot seem to
> grasp the fact that we are now alone and at the
> mercy of those we hired to guide us. I've had to

warn him again and again about his brutality to
the natives. God keep us from having our throats
cut some moonless night!

Thorson read the passage over again. He had no
memory of Absalom Wish, but he'd pictured the
man as another Huntley Drew and this account of
him stood in startling contrast to his conception.
Skimming through more pages, he learned that
there'd been constant friction between the two
archeologists, and then this passage took his attention:

Ab is down with fever and raved away most of
the night. He talked about the old days in California, and I must confess that I led him on with
pointed questions. And it is as I have feared all
these years. He *was* the man behind that atrocity
in the Sierraville diggings. He admitted it in his
delirium. And yet I'm not surprised. Perhaps I
turned my back on most of the evidence in the old
days. And probably I sinned in doing so. I should
have remembered my duty as a vigilante and forgotten that he and I were colleagues and that he
was Louise's brother. God forgive me for that.

Again Thorson turned the pages, reading of exca-
vations that had uncovered Mayan sacrificial pools
and the remains of the paved highways that had
connected the forty-odd cities of that ancient and
long-forgotten empire.
And then:

Ab is up and about and we have decided to call
off the expedition and return to the States. He did
very little arguing. The fever still has a grip on
him, and he'd like to get to competent doctors. I
can't help wondering what goes on in his mind.

Many times I've felt his eyes upon me, and my fear is that he partly remembers that night when I quizzed him in his delirium.

There was more, but Thorson didn't find it interesting and at last he put the book aside, restoring it and the envelope to the trunk. Spinning a cigarette, he smoked thoughtfully, wondering if he had the answer to a riddle. But he couldn't be sure one way or another, so he blew out the lamp and went downstairs and out of the house into the first pale flush of morning.

He was tired, extremely tired. The fight with Fee and the manifold excitements of the night had taken a stern toll. But he spurred himself onward, heading along the gulch to the diggings and coming to the shack of Zeke Lockhart before anybody was astir. Lockhart was asleep, but not for long. He awoke at the first pressure of Thorson's hand, blinking and staring about.

"Sorry, Zeke," Thorson said. "My business couldn't wait. I can't do much explaining; I can only ask that you do as I say—without any questions. How about it?"

Lockhart knuckled the sleep from his eyes.

"I'm listening," he said.

"I want you to get about a dozen vigilantes together. I'd do it myself, but I want to be back at the house before I'm found missing. That's one of the things I can't tell you about. When you get your boys, string six of them around the stone house. Their job will be to keep under cover, and to make damn' sure that Matthew Fee doesn't leave. The other six will keep an eye on Belle Kincaid's cabin."

"Kincaid's? But I don't understand—!"

Thorson measured him with a thoughtful look. "I'll let you in on one secret, Zeke," he said. "If I didn't think you could keep it, I wouldn't be here getting your help. When I brought you along with me to the Kincaid cabin to get Rory last night, I didn't tell you how I knew he'd be there. It was Belle Kincaid who put Rory O'Doone into our hands. And now Rory's loose. I think he was too drunk to be sure that Miss Kincaid betrayed him, but I can't be certain about that. So we've got to keep her protected. Now will you get at it?"

It was Lockhart's turn to do some studying, and then he said, "Good enough, Tod. You're trusting me; I'm trusting you. I'll have the boys on the job right away."

"Thanks," said Thorson and left the shack.

He came back up through the diggings, heading in the direction of the stone house, and part of the way brought him wending through heaps of tailings, high as a man and higher. And what happened here was partly because weariness had taken the edge from his alertness, and partly because the men who awaited him had seen him coming and planned their moves with care. He never saw the one who hit him. The fellow came from behind and to one side, easing out from the cover of one of those black piles, and Thorson's first intimation of his presence was when a gun-barrel caught him along the side of his head.

He went down, a curtain of blood dropping to blind him, and it was a hard fight to hold on to consciousness in that swirling moment. He had a glimpse of the four men who came crowding around him, recognizing them as Charlie Wagner and the Strunk brothers and Rory O'Doone. Down on his hands and knees, Thorson tried to come erect again, but the strength wasn't in him. Wagner said, "He's bleeding bad, but he sure isn't dead. I'll put a bullet in him."

"And have the diggings swarming with miners?" O'Doone snapped. "No, you fool! Give him another

clout and pack him over to Tom Conway's old shaft.
It ain't far. Heave him down the shaft, and if the fall
don't kill him he'll lay and bleed to death before he's
found. Hurry it up!"

"You can give us a hand, can't you?"

"I've got other business," said Rory. "I'll meet
you where we left the horses. Then you'll catch on
why I had us get an extra mount. Me, I'm calling on
a lady."

Again Thorson made his desperate effort to come
to his feet. But he wouldn't have succeeded, even if
Wagner's gun-barrel hadn't risen and fallen again,
driving him deep into the blackness of oblivion. . . .

Belle Kincaid, like Ginny Drew and many another, had gotten no sleep this night. After Tod Thorson had left her outside the stone house, Belle had
made her solitary way back to her own cabin, coming into it and leaving the door open behind her and
shoving back the one window, for the sour smell of
whiskey permeated the place, a sickening reek.
Finding a seat beside the window, she sat staring
into the darkness, thinking of many things.

Tonight she'd played Delilah to a malignant Sam-
son, and she found neither satisfaction nor regret as
she considered the ultimate fate of Rory O'Doone.
The man had denied being the murderer of Jamieson Hazzard. Considering the circumstances that
had prompted his denial, she had had to believe
him. Therefore O'Doone counted for nothing in her
scheme of things. One need and one alone had kept
her in Thunder Gulch, and that was the need to
avenge the man she'd come too late to marry.
O'Doone was a murderer, but not the murderer she
sought. Turning him over to the vigilantes was
something that would have pleased Pi Hazzard, so

she'd played the cards accordingly. But her real work remained unfinished.

And when it was done, when she'd found the man who had brought Hazzard to his death, what then? That was something she'd never considered, and she refused to consider it now. She had died that same morning Hazzard had died, and she'd lived since only because she'd found this single need for living. She did not care to look beyond the fulfillment of that need.

O'Doone had mentioned the name of Matthew Fee. Tomorrow she would try tracking a truth to Fee's door. That was the one thing that mattered; she had to be very, very sure.

And so she whiled away the long hours, hearing the measured tread of the men who came to the cottonwood below the stone house, a faint, faraway sound without interest for her. Once she wondered if Rory O'Doone were dead, and if he'd suspected the truth about her before he'd died. And after a long time she discovered she was cold and that the morning had begun to come. Closing the window and the door, she put out the lamp and was about to undress for bed when the door opened and Rory O'Doone came into the cabin.

He said, "You sure as hell look surprised. But I can't say that you look a damn' bit pleased!"

Backing against the wall, she put her hand to her mouth, but she didn't scream.

"I—I thought they'd hung you!" she said.

"So you *did* know about that!" he snarled and fury turned his crescent-shaped scar to a flaming crimson. "You turned me over to them, didn't you? But I got away, and I'm back. I seem to remember promising to show you a road agent shebang down the Old South Road. But your vigilante friends raided it tonight. But there's another shebang at Michigan Hole. You've made this camp too hot for me and I'm heading there, and you're going with me! You're going along because I can't take the chance of killing you here and now! Do you understand me, you she-Judas!''

She reached for the derringer in her dress front and got it into her hand, but he was upon her at once, wrenching the tiny gun away and flinging it over his shoulder. Breaking free of him, she made a wild and frantic dash toward the door, but he was too quick for her, grasping at her arm. The whiskey gone out of him, he was grim and terrible in his sobriety and his anger, and there was no escaping him and no matching his strength.

Chapter Sixteen
ROAD AGENT RENDEZVOUS

As Charlie Wagner and the Strunk brothers came carrying Tod Thorson, limp and unconscious, toward the dark, yawning mouth of Tom Conway's abandoned shaft, they moved as swiftly as they could, mindful that the morning was here and that the noose they'd so narrowly escaped would still claim them if they were caught at this grim and furtive task. Thad Strunk cursed softly and said, "Why couldn't Rory have lent a hand? Who'd think a jigger Thorson's size would be so heavy to tote?"

"We're almost there," Wagner panted. "A few more steps and a heave and he's down at the bottom of the shaft. And then there's one less vigilante."

Moving through a littered maze of heaped tailings, stepping over discarded sluice boxes that had been hauled here and left to crumble, they were a dozen paces nearer their destination when the other Strunk brother, Zack, straightened abruptly, letting go of one of Thorson's legs. "Over yonder, beyond that pile of tailings!" he cried. "I saw someone moving!"

"Your nerves are jumpy," Wagner scoffed. But he let Thorson's shoulders hit the ground, and he put his hand to the gun at his hip, but he didn't have a chance to draw it.

They came from everywhere, the men who swarmed down upon the road agent trio. They came on soundless feet, disgorging from the last of the shadows and from every kind of cover, a silent, sweeping fury. Black alpaca swished, the new day's light put a sheen on darting knives, and Charlie Wagner made a low and throaty sound as he died beneath a blade. Zack Strunk fell writhing across Wagner's body, and Thad Strunk only had time to gasp, *"Chinks!"* and make a wild and futile try for his gun before the life went out of him, too. That was the way it happened, the whole of it so quickly that it took far less than a minute's time.

There was one who could only stand back while the skirmish lasted, a tall, round-shouldered man whose hands were hidden in the voluminous sleeves of his padded silk jacket and whose dim eyes quested the distance, seeing nothing but blurred, shadowy movements. He stood waiting until a younger Chinese came and made a shrill report. Then Quong Lee said in the tongue of his people, "Carry him to my poor house."

A dozen hands were put to the task, and Thorson was brought to the Chinese end of the diggings and into the shack of Quong Lee. Here he was stretched upon a bed, the nimble fingers of Quong Lee acting as eyes for the Chinese as he went about examining Thorson's scalp wound and caring for it. And thus it was that Thorson soon opened his eyes to stare in surprise, finding Quong Lee bending over him.

"Sleep," advised Quong Lee. "Is no need to worry. In my own land I stored up learning, hoping to be great physician."

Finding himself here when he should have been at the bottom of Conway's shaft was astonishing enough to Thorson; learning that Quong Lee possessed medicinal talents was even more astonishing. He had a lot of questions crowding his tongue, but he only said, "Good enough, old son." And went to sleep.

Hours later he opened his eyes again and was hard put to recognize his whereabouts until the incongruity of his surroundings gave him a key to memory. Rude shacks Thunder Gulch had in plenty, but this was the first Thorson had seen with teak furniture and multicolored lanterns. On one wall hung a scroll, on another a picture painted on silk, while a shelf held a row of books, English language classics all of them. The most familiar sight to Thorson's eyes was the tall figure of Dr. Drew, who sat hunched by his bedside.

"Hello," Tod said. "How long have I slept?"

"It's nearly noon," Dr. Drew told him. "Quong sent for me in the middle of the morning, but we let you sleep. Quong constantly grows more amazing. Did you know that he was a physician? He did as competent a job of caring for your scalp wound as any I ever saw. More than that, he perhaps saved the lives of all of us. When we roused the vigilantes last night, I had one fetch word to Quong. His first move was to send his Chinese out through the gulch to act as eyes and ears. Quong was afraid that while we were hanging some of the road agents, the rest might get wind of our move and strike at us. He was making sure that didn't happen. That's how he and some of his people happened to be on hand when Wagner and the Strunks waylaid you. Quong told me all about it."

"Rory O'Doone!" Thorson cried in sudden remembrance. "And Belle Kincaid! Rory was going after her while those other three were getting rid of me!"

Drew's head jerked. "So that's it! Belle's gone, Tod. Zeke Lockhart came to the stone house looking for you, shortly after dawn. He'd roused some vigilantes to keep an eye on Belle's cabin, but when they got there, the cabin was empty. It looked like there'd been a struggle. I've got men out in the hills now, hunting for Belle."

Thorson sank back, sick with dismay. "He got her!" he said. "He reached the cabin ahead of the guards! What a fool I was to have let her go back there!"

Quong Lee padded into the room and placed a hand on Thorson's forehead. Disappearing into an adjoining room, he returned with some vile-tasting herb medicine which he spooned into his patient.

This doctoring finished, Quong Lee put his shoulders to the wall and made a silent, unobtrusive figure.

"I suppose you're wondering how I got into trouble," Thorson said. "I'm the one who sent Zeke to get guards for Belle. After I left his shack, Wagner and the Strunks and O'Doone jumped me. They were going to dump me down Conway's shaft, and they must have been toting me when the Chinese came along."

Drew nodded, his face grave. "Because of O'Doone, you were nearly murdered, and now Belle is O'Doone's prisoner. And it's all my fault, Tod. I'm going to tell you the truth. I *let* Rory O'Doone escape!"

Even if that wasn't news, it was still a great surprise, and Thorson made no effort to hide his astonishment. "I'd like to know why," he said.

"And you've got a right to know, and so has Quong," Drew said. "O'Doone was in the California diggings year ago when I was there. After I'd seen him at the miner's election, I remembered him, and, considering the way his jaw fell when I was named, it would seem that he remembered me, too. Why he came to rummage through my luggage that night, I don't know. Possibly he was looking for valuables. But in any case, he had a look at my diary."

"I had a look at it myself," Thorson admitted. "You're facing your cards, so I'll face mine. Ginny told me what she'd overheard in the hallway. You can't blame her for it, Drew. She didn't want to believe you were a turncoat, but she hadn't much choice. So I got curious as to what Rory had found in your trunk that gave him a club over you."

"And you saw the passages about Absalom Wish and what he really was?"

Thorson nodded.

"Then you've probably guessed all the truth. Absalom Wish was a man with a dual nature—a great scientist on the one hand, a cold-blooded ruffian on the other. Quong, if you don't already know, you might as well know now: It was Ab Wish who led the raid on the Chinese diggings out of Sierraville the night you almost lost your eyes."

"Truth apparent to me for many years," Quong said softly.

"And to me, also," Drew went on. "The vigilantes investigated that little episode, and most of the evidence came to my attention. God forgive me for being blind to what I didn't want to see! But the proof wasn't conclusive, and I saw to it that Ab was never prosecuted. My reasons were two. First, he was kin, my wife's brother. And secondly, I still couldn't quite reconcile the idea that Absalom Wish, outstanding archeologist, was also Absalom Wish, road agent and leader of road agents. Actually I never had the full truth till he talked in his delirium down in Yucatán. Ab died from the fever he contracted there. As I see it, his case went to a Higher Court than any I might have brought him before."

"And Rory learned the truth about him from your diary?"

"He did. Rory was in on that Sierraville raid, but he'd never been sure as to the real identity of the leader. Ab was careful in such matters, but Rory had had his suspicions all these years. My diary told enough to confirm his suspicions. Last night, when Rory sent for me, he told me what he knew. He'd written down his information and passed it along to a friend, he claimed. If he died, that paper was to be mailed to a San Francisco newspaper. Do you see what that would mean?"

"The blackening of Absalom Wish's name," Thorson said.

"And who'd be hurt by that?" Drew demanded. "Virginia, for one. After all, she's Ab's niece and she's had no inkling of the truth about him. And a name that stands high in archeology would be remembered only as the name of a criminal. No, Tod, I couldn't do that to Ginny, or to the memory of the scientist Ab Wish was. Rory was scared stiff last night, as you know. If I turned him loose, I felt that he'd leave and never show himself again. I didn't know I was freeing him to try murdering you and to kidnap Belle. But the damage is done, the fault is mine, and now you have the truth."

"I found four names written on the back of an envelope," Thorson said. "Lars Thorson, Jamieson Hazzard, Quong Lee and Rory O'Doone. Three were crossed out; Rory's had question marks after it."

"I wrote those names," Drew said. "I jotted them down absently one evening after O'Doone had rummaged through my luggage. I was trying to recall how many men in Thunder Gulch might possibly have known the truth about Ab and that Sierraville raid, and there were four. Three I crossed out, because they were men of integrity who'd have helped keep the secret. The fourth, O'Doone, was the one who was a question."

He held silent then, his glance humble and appealing, and Thorson found the judgment seat an uneasy one, but his greatest reaction was jubilation, and that was because of Ginny. "I've a confession too," he said. "I told Lockhart to put guards around Belle's cabin, but I also told him to see that a watch was kept on Matthew Fee. Perhaps you can understand why."

"You thought I might be playing hand-in-glove with all the road agents," Drew nodded. "I can't blame either you or Virginia for your suspicions. I think I shall tell her the truth, too, Tod. That will be the best way. And we're trying Matthew Fee this afternoon in the miner's court building. All Thunder Gulch can come if it wants. You'll be on your feet by then, I hope."

"You bet I will," Thorson said.

Drew looked at Quong Lee. "I've made my peace with Thorson, and I'll make it with my daughter. But what about you, Quong? The man who did you harm might have been hanged years ago if I hadn't closed one eye to my duty. I've told you how it was, and I hope that you understand."

There was no seeing through the inscrutability of Quong Lee. "Recently read quotation comes to mind," he said. " 'Though the mills of God grind slowly, yet they grind exceeding small . . .' Is true, Doctor?"

Rory O'Doone had come out of Belle Kincaid's cabin with the woman in his arms, a writhing, squirming burden bound hand and foot and gagged as well. He carried her to where five waiting horses were hidden behind a rocky upthrust on the gulch's south slope, and here he loosened her feet, but only long enough to heave her aboard a horse and lash her there.

Three of these horses belonged to Charlie Wagner and the Strunk brothers and had been given back to them by the vigilantes; the other two had been stolen from the livery stable less than an hour before, and they'd been selected with an eye to speed and bottom. Climbing into the saddle of a big roan, Rory waited impatiently for the coming of his friends. When his final estimate on time and distance proved them to be long overdue, he gave up his vigil, riding off and leading Belle's horse after him.

He had one last glimpse of the gulch before the

turn to a bushy draw, cutting back into the slope,
put it beyond his sight, and his last look was at that
giant cottonwood and the three swaying figures he'd
betrayed, stark against the first light. He took his
eyes away quickly and rode onward, driving deeper
into the hilly country that lay to the south of the
gulch. After a half hour's riding, he removed the gag
from Belle's mouth and used the cloth to blindfold
her. "Holler all you want," he told her. "The only
answer you'll get is your echo."

She said, "I wouldn't give you that much satisfaction!" The scorn in her voice drew his mouth to a
tight line, and he promised himself that he'd find a
way to change her attitude before this day was
through. But now he put all his faculties to the finding of a hidden trail. The road agents had a secret
route through here, and he had to watch for tiny
markings on trees and a dozen scattered signs that
pointed the way. Within another hour or so he was
facing a sheer precipice which loomed high above
him, but it took considerable searching before he
found a certain mammoth boulder and the rift behind it, a crevice so narrow that it crowded the
horses.

This was the Michigan Hole hideout. Michigan
men had come to this part of Montana long ago,
done some futile scratching and gone their way,
leaving the fabulous Thunder Gulch diggings to be
found by another man in the years to come. But
those Michiganders had left their mark on the map.
It was they who'd called the barrier mountains the
Wolverines, and they'd given the name to Michigan
Creeks and Michigan Hills as reminders of their
brief stay. And Michigan Hole, long forgotten by
most, still bore the name of its discoverers.

It was a natural pocket, a wide, grass-carpeted
bowl, canopied by a stretch of blue sky and walled
by cliffs within a cliff. Close up under these inner

cliffs was a scattering of cabins, and O'Doone dismounted before one, dragging Belle from her saddle and toting her inside. He thrust her into a lean-to, jerked the blindfold from her eyes and stirred her with the toe of his boot. "I'm getting some sleep," he said. "Maybe you'll wriggle out of those ropes, but I don't think so. And you'd play hell trying to find your way back to Thunder Gulch."

Closing the door to the lean-to, he threw himself upon a bunk, and he'd gotten a few hours' sleep when he was aroused by the thud of hoofs. He'd borrowed a gun from one of the Strunks, and it was in his hand as he edged to the door of the cabin. But the half-dozen men who were dismounting were all known to him, and he found them a tight-lipped, sullen bunch.

"There's hell to pay in the gulch," Sooner Dobbs reported, he who'd once blistered his feet on the slant of Wolverine Pass after Thorson had taken a wagon away from him. "Jake DeSpain passed the word for us to meet here. That was Matt Fee's idea. But I reckon it will be Matt's last order. The vigilantes have got him."

That was news to Rory O'Doone. "They had me, too," he said. "I got away. And I fetched the Kincaid woman along with me. She's the one who told the vigilantes about the South Road shebang."

Dobbs said, "A lot of good having her is gonna do us. The vigilantes are out now, beating the brush for sign of her. You're a damn' fool, O'Doone."

"We'll see," Rory said and lifted his eyes toward the rift in the wall. "Look, some more of the boys are coming."

And they were only a few of many who were to come that day, for Jake DeSpain had passed the word and all the road agent legion was slowly gathering at this rendezvous. The number increasing, there was much damning of the vigilantes and much talk of reprisal, and Rory, listening, wondered how long his life would last if these men knew he'd been the one who'd betrayed Doheny, Lucas and Pease to their death and put Matthew Fee into vigilante hands.

That last was the one thing Rory really regretted, and his regret grew with the passing hours and was not made from any workings of his conscience. Here was the strength of the road agents gathering, but where was the man to point the way and to lead them? There was a need for Matthew Fee as there'd never been before, and no man felt it more keenly than Rory O'Doone. And in the early afternoon there came word of Matthew Fee. Jake DeSpain was the one who fetched it.

"They're putting Fee on trial this afternoon," the houseman said as he swung down from his horse. "They're holding public trial and all the gulch will be on hand. Your money will get you any kind of bet in Thunder Gulch that Matt will be dangling by sundown."

A full fifty road agents were here now, and Rory measured the collective strength of them and said, "Maybe we could snatch him from the rope."

"And be cut to doll ribbons by their guns," DeSpain scoffed. "The vigilantes aren't so many, but once that trial is over and the town sees that Matt Fee isn't half as wide across the britches as they'd thought, every man in camp will be ready to back the Thorson crowd. Did you hear that Charlie Wagner and the Strunk boys were stabbed to death by a bunch of Chinks? They caught the boys toting Thorson toward Tom Conway's old shaft. And the vigilantes are wild about Belle Kincaid being packed off. The talk is that you did that job, Rory. If you've got her here, I'm saying you'd better turn her loose —and right now!"

But Rory O'Doone had become possessed of a

vast and startling idea, and he looked into the sunken eyes of Jake DeSpain and said, "You'll be going back to camp, won't you, Jake? You're safe enough there. Then tote a note along for me, and maybe they won't be hanging Matt Fee after all! The boys think I'm loco for bringing the woman here, but they're wrong. She's going to be the best ace-in-the-hole we ever had!"

Chapter Seventeen
THE GOLD GOES OUT

They fetched Matthew Fee from the stone house in the late afternoon, the bell booming atop the miner's court building and all Thunder Gulch agog with the excitement of this significant day. The diggings had been deserted since early morning, for the news had gotten around, leaving a tingling tension in its wake.

There were men in the street, scores of them, making small talk and loud talk, doing much drinking and laying many bets. There were men on the trail up the slant, and men in the meeting hall, come hours early to get the best seats.

They brought Fee across the shoulder of the slope, and he walked along stiffly erect, hiding the run of his thoughts with a sullen air of indifference. But when he looked down toward the cottonwood where three men had been left hanging until an hour ago, Fee stumbled, swallowed hard and looked elsewhere. Dr. Drew was in the group escorting him, and so were the six vigilantes Zeke Lockhart had posted as guards, and Tod Thorson was along too, his head bandaged but his step steady enough to testify to Quong Lee's skill as a physician. When they thrust Fee into the meeting hall, the big man blinked in the darkness, looking for faces that weren't here, and a seated miner cried shrilly, "Here's the dirty killer now!"

Fee spread his feet in the aisle and glared at the man. "Yesterday any of you mealymouthed sons would have jumped out of your skins if I'd shouted 'Boo!'" he said. "You'd better wait till I'm safely hanged before you call me names!"

A guard nudged him on up to the front of the room, and Zeke Lockhart moved from the bell rope to the raised platform, lifting his hands. "All of you know we're holding a trial," he said. "And all of you know that three men were hanged last night. That was the work of a group of us who banded together to bring law to these diggin's. We're hoping that our work will be finished today, and that Thunder Gulch will no longer need vigilantes. But that's up to the town. And that's why we're expecting every man of you to listen to the evidence and decide whether this man hangs or goes free."

Fee said, "What am I accused of? Or is that a vigilante secret?"

Lockhart singled out Thorson with his eyes. "You talked to Rory O'Doone last night, Tod. Tell the court what he had to say about Fee."

More miners came filtering into the room, making a great deal of commotion as they found seats, and a group of Chinese padded in at their heels and strung out across the back of the room. After that it grew quiet again and Thorson spoke. "We were going to hang Rory for Thiebault's death," he said. "I asked him if he'd also killed Hazzard. He blamed that on Fee, said Fee was the road agent boss and had a hundred hangings coming to him. And he mentioned Eph Tutt's name."

A mutter swept the room, and fierce anger colored Fee's battered face. "Anything else?" he asked.

"We've got a list here as long as your arm," said Lockhart. "There's the second marshal of Thunder Gulch, the one who died in the alley behind your Hurdy-Gurdy House. And there's Thiebault too. Harry Pease confessed that you got a cut of Frenchy's dust, even if you weren't in on the actual killing. And there's the evidence that you put a torch to the *Trumpet* building and left Thorson to die.

Have you forgotten the printer's ink you got smeared on your hand that night? And there's that valise you packed last night, Fee. We've had a look in it, and we found a few pokes of gold dust along with the folding money. Those pokes were initialed. They belonged to Eph Tutt, who was tortured until he told where his gold was hidden, then killed!"

"You're talking about suspicions," Fee scoffed. "Where's real evidence?"

A miner bounced to his feet crying, "I've got something to say!" Looking at him, Thorson saw a mousy little man whom he'd seen around the diggings but had never met. Here was one who hadn't come to join the vigilantes, but he'd borrowed a measure of their courage.

"I crossed near Eph Tutt's shack the night of the trouble, though I didn't hear what had happened to Eph till the next day," the miner said. "I saw three masked men come moving out of the shadows, so I stretched myself out behind an old sluice box. I wasn't five feet from 'em when they took off their masks. Fee was one of 'em, Joe Coulter, who drives a freight wagon for him sometimes, was another, and O'Doone was the third. Fee said, 'It isn't much for an hour's hard work, but we'll divide the dust later. Who'd think that old coot would be so stubborn?'"

Thorson got in a word. "Why didn't you tell this as soon as you heard about Tutt being murdered?" he asked.

The miner looked from him to Fee and back again, then colored quickly. "I was afraid," he said and sat down.

And that was when it came to Thorson that here was the greatest victory the vigilantes had won, and the thought was big and lifting, for a man who'd been afraid was no longer afraid. Thus had the might of Matthew Fee been proved a thing made out of shadow, and there was a sudden wild clamoring in the court, a great flourishing of fists, and a throaty rumble rose crying, "Lynch him! Drag him down to the cottonwood and give him a taste of the rope!"

Zeke Lockhart rapped long and hard for order and, getting a measure of it, made himself heard. "There'll be none of that!" he said sternly. "We'll take a vote. If the vote goes against him he dies, but not otherwise. Fee, have you got anything to say for yourself?"

Matthew Fee seemed to have lost inches in this last moment, and Thorson was suddenly afraid that the man was going to crumble and be as Rory O'Doone had been, cowering and abject and loathsome. He couldn't have told why, but he was glad when Fee threw back his shoulders and faced the crowd with a show of truculence.

"I know when a game's gone against me," Fee said. "I'm going to ask a favor, and when I do, I want you to remember this: You're as right as rain, all of you. I'm a dozen times guilty, for I'm the man who's been behind the road agents. You vigilantes haven't made a mistake yet, and you're not making one now. And to hell with the whole bunch of you! But before I'm hung, will you give me fifteen minutes alone in a room with Rory, if he isn't already dead?"

Lockhart said, "You've probably got that much coming to you, Fee. But O'Doone got away on us. Gentlemen, are you ready to vote? If you figger this man's guilty say 'Aye.' "

The response was thunderous, leaving no shadow of a doubt, and thus was Matthew Fee doomed by all of Thunder Gulch, and Lockhart said, "We'll build some sort of gallows this afternoon. Fee, as head of the miner's court and executive officer of the Thunder Gulch vigilantes, I sentence you to be hanged at sundown."

Fee was thrust down the aisle, Thorson falling in with the armed escort, and Fee looked at him and smiled a tight and humorless smile. "Once you told me you'd run me out of the diggings," Fee said. "I leave at sundown, Thorson. Are you satisfied now?"

Thorson shook his head. "Our fight finished in your office last night," Thorson said. "What happened today wasn't a personal matter. I want you to know that, Fee. Twice that I can remember, you offered me your hand, and both times I refused it because you didn't mean the gesture. If it wasn't for Jamieson Hazzard, I'd be willing to take it now."

Fee's smiled faded. "Thorson, I hate your guts," he said. "I hate you because I've had a hunch from the start that you'd be the finishing of me. That's why I sent Rory to waylay Josh Hoskins' coach and try and kill you before you reached Thunder Gulch. Yeah, I'm admitting that, too. But I never killed Pi Hazzard. That's why I wanted that fifteen minutes with Rory O'Doone."

"Then," said Thorson, "at sundown Thunder Gulch will be paid off; but I won't."

"And I'll be laughing at you," Fee said.

They brought him back to Lars Thorson's house and locked him in that same upstairs room, and the head men of the vigilantes gathered in the living room, Dr. Drew, Thorson and Pat Shea among them. Lockhart came bustling in shortly afterwards. "I've started some of the boys building a gallows," he said. "The temper of the town is bad, but I don't think there'll be any lynch play."

"Or any rescue," Shea remarked. "Have you noticed that there isn't a Fee man around camp? Even his stamp mill crew is gone. I think we'll be moving our gold to Benton within a week. Once the news gets into the hills that Fee is dead, there won't be a road agent this side of the Wolverines."

"Supposing O'Doone bands them together?" Lockhart said.

Shea made a quick and derisive gesture. "O'Doone's no good without Fee to do his thinking for him. The quickest way to kill a snake is to cut off its head. That's what we'll be doing at sundown."

"Somebody coming down the hall," Dr. Drew observed.

It was Cory, the vigilante guard of last night, and with him was a tall, flat-chested man with a lean, cadaverous face.

Thorson looked in astonishment and said, "Where did you find him, Cory? He's one of Fee's housemen."

"He claims he's here under a flag of truce," Cory said. "He's got a note for the vigilantes."

Jake DeSpain shifted uneasily from one foot to another, his fear naked in his eyes. "I was just asked to pass it along," he said.

He extended a folded piece of paper to Dr. Drew, and the blood faded from Drew's face as he read it, and he was older when he'd finished. Silently he passed the paper to Thorson, and Lockhart said, "Read it aloud, man! For Pete's sake, read it!"

"It's from O'Doone," Thorson noticed. "It says, 'We know what you figger on doing, but while you're getting ready to hang Fee, just remember that we can build a gallows too. At the same moment that Matt dangles, we hang Belle Kincaid. Or are you maybe interested in a swap?'"

A vigilante over beside the fireplace began cursing in a low and steady voice, and Drew said, "Cory, take that walking cadaver somewhere beyond earshot, and keep him under your gun. We've got a council to hold."

Cory was walking DeSpain down the hall when

Shea said, "So that's the size of it! An eye for an eye, and a tooth for a tooth! And I say to hell with 'em! Why should we spare Fee's neck for the sake of some dance-hall hussy?"

Drew, sunk deep in his chair, looked to Thorson for help. "Tell him, Tod; tell him!" Drew said in a stricken voice.

"Pat, you don't understand," Thorson said softly. "Belle Kincaid was working for Fee in order to get information. She's the one who started us riding last night. The vigilantes would still be twirling their thumbs, waiting a chance to strike, if it hadn't been for her. That's why O'Doone hates her, and that's why he carried her off. And we've no choice, Pat. No choice at all."

Shea took to pacing the room. "I didn't know about that," he said. "But we had our work finished —finished, do you understand! And suppose we turn Fee loose? We can banish him, of course, but he'll hide out in the hills with his bunch. What chance will we have to get our gold out then?"

"We're not thinking about the gold, Pat."

Shea flushed. "I'm sorry, Tod. Like all the rest, I've been waiting so long to get that gold moving that I've lost sight of everything else. We don't need to hold any council. Doctor, hadn't you better get a note off to O'Doone?"

Thorson got pen and ink, and Drew dictated a note which read: "We are willing to release Fee on the following terms: Belle Kincaid must first be freed and returned to the gulch within an hour after sundown. Upon her appearance, Fee will be escorted to any point you designate, turned loose and given twenty-four hours to get moving. From that time on, he and all the rest of you will be fair game. You have our solemn promise that our end of the bargain will be kept."

They all put their signatures to the note, and De-

Spain was called back into the room. "Get this to the man who sent you here," Drew said. "After that, you'd better keep heading whichever direction you were going!"

DeSpain gone from the house, Shea said, "So we don't cut off the snake's head after all! We'd better keep this quiet. If the news gets out that Fee may be spared, the town might try lynching him."

"I'll keep the boys working at the gallows," Lockhart decided. "Folks would wonder if we quit building it."

All of them fell silent then, for victory had turned into defeat by virtue of Rory O'Doone's desperate play, and the taste of defeat was bitter. Thorson began pacing, busy with his thoughts, but after a minute he broke stride abruptly. "I've got it!" he said. "The gold *can* go out! Tonight!"

Shea's eyes lighted, but only briefly. "With the hills crawling with road agents?" he scoffed.

"Look at it this way!" Thorson said. "They won't be expecting us to make any such move till we've got them chased out of the country. They'll be holed up somewhere, waiting for Fee's return. And we'll be on our way to Benton before they find out what we're doing!"

"And they'll come up Wolverine Pass as fast as horses can carry them," Shea put in. "Ore wagons roll slow, Tod."

"Let 'em come over Wolverine! We'll send the treasure train down the Old South Road. It's a longer way and a harder way, I'm told. But it was used before the Wolverine Pass route was put through, and it can be used again. Who'd ever suspect us of going that way?"

Some of them began to stir with interest, and Shea's skepticism took its first turn toward enthusiasm. "But a few of Fee's bunch are probably still in the gulch," he said. "Fellows like that DeSpain, for instance. We'll have to play it careful."

"And we will! We'll send the wagons out one by one, and have them line up in the canyon down the Old South Road till the whole train is assembled. Vigilantes can ride along as guards. Doctor, what do you think of it?"

"It might work," Drew said slowly. "In fact, I believe it will! Freighters come through from Lewiston constantly, on their way to Benton. If we're cautious enough, a few more wagons on the street won't be noticed. Will you tool ours, Tod?"

"No, Shea can handle it," Thorson decided. "I'll overtake the train later. I want to stay here till I'm sure that Belle has been turned loose."

"Then the rest of us had better get busy," Shea said.

Thus was the plan made, and after the miners had dribbled out of the house, there was much furtive activity in the diggings, but for Thorson the rest of the afternoon dragged by to the tune of pounding hammers and rasping saws as the gallows went up in the shadow of the miner's court building. He took frequent trips to the *Trumpet* office, where Ginny toiled at writing the news of the last day and night, and he bobbed into the various bars, listening to the talk of the town and returning to report it to Dr. Drew, who waited alone in the stone house.

The sun dipping to the west, the vigilantes who'd gone scouring the hills for sign of Belle Kincaid returned to report a fruitless search. They were sent to the diggings to help with the loading of the treasure train, and so were the six who kept guard on Matthew Fee. Lockhart came to the house from time to time, telling of the secret progress that was being made, and Thorson, the first flush of his enthusiasm passing, heard him out and wondered whether his plan was as tight as he'd intended it to be. But the die was cast, and the gold was going out.

Then sundown came, the gallows was finished, but there was no hanging, the vigilantes spreading word through the camp that Fee's execution had been postponed pending certain events. Speculation sped on fanciful wings, Thunder Gulch watching and waiting and inventing a hundred wild theories to explain the delay. Thus, with excitement singing in the air, there were few to heed the sullen rumble of wagons or to speculate upon their passing or to note the route they took. And the deepening shadows matched the dark and somber mood of Thorson as he waited for whatever the night would bring.

Chapter Eighteen
LONG TRAIL'S ENDING

Two riders had left Michigan Hole in the last of the day's light, the man hunched low in his saddle, the woman tied to hers and blindfolded once again. The shadows were thronging when they came to the bushy draw south of Thunder Gulch, and it was here that Rory O'Doone hauled his horse to a stand and stepped down to the ground with a quick and nervous movement. He had a knife, a less ornate one than the silver-inlaid bowie Zeke Lockhart had taken from him, and he used it to saw Belle Kincaid free of the ropes.

Whisking her blindfold away, he said, "Just follow this draw and you'll come out into the gulch. I've told you the setup, and I'm expecting a fair deal from the vigilantes. Matt Fee will know where to find me once he's turned loose."

For a woman who'd brushed with death and come through unscathed, she showed no elation. Her handsome face was drawn with bitterness. "If I could have gotten word to the vigilantes, they'd have struck no such bargain with you," she said. "Anything you might have done to me wouldn't have mattered if Fee had hanged at sundown. He was the one who killed Hazzard, wasn't he?"

He made no answer, but she could see the hatred in his eyes, and she knew how much it had cost him to forgo the revenge he might have had. Also, she could see that it put a nervous tension in him to be this close to Thunder Gulch. Coming up into his saddle quickly, he said, "You'd better get going."

She gave him a smile at parting, but she hadn't intended it and she hoped he wouldn't guess what had suddenly lifted her spirits. Scowling, he said, "Get that thought out of your head! You'd like to fade back into these hills and have the vigilantes think that we weren't turning you loose. That way, they'd go ahead and hang Matt. But I'll be following along and keeping an eye on you till you're well into the camp. You'll never work that kind of double-cross. Now git!"

He might be bluffing, and she rather suspected that he was, for she couldn't quite picture him tagging her into the camp. Yet he could do it safely enough. The vigilantes would consider this an armed truce, so long as he was fetching her to them. Her shoulders slumped again as her quick-born scheme went winging, and she nudged her horse and rode slowly up the draw until she came out onto the south slope of Thunder Gulch, the camp sprawling below her. Taking a glance behind her, she could see nothing but shadows. But she thought she heard the cautious creak of saddle leather and she shrugged in surrender, riding on down into the gulch and coming between two buildings to the thronged street.

There was more traffic than she remembered from other nights, and a heavy ore wagon rumbled past her, the driver looking down from his high perch and swearing in his astonishment. "It's Miss Kincaid, ain't it?" he asked. "When did you get back to the camp?"

This was Pat Shea, but she'd never known the overseer of the discovery claim, and she could only presume that all of Thunder Gulch's citizenry had been watching and waiting for her. She said, "I just arrived. Could you tell me where I'd likely find Dr. Drew or Tod Thorson?"

"Doc's up at the stone house," Shea said. "I saw Thorson on the street a moment ago. Look, there he is yonder in the *Trumpet* office."

Across the way she could see the lighted log building, its window giving her a glimpse of Ginny at the desk and Thorson standing near her, talking and gesticulating. She knew now that there'd be no hiding the truth that she'd been freed, so as Shea's wagon moved on toward the east, she nudged her horse over to the nearest hitchrail, the one in front of the Empire House.

She was down out of the saddle and wrapping the reins about the gnawed bar when another wagon came to a squealing stop in the street. A high-sided freighter, it had the name of a Lewiston trading company lettered on it, and a man who'd been seated beside the driver was climbing off the wagon, clutching his luggage to him. "Ah, there, Miss Kincaid," he said in surprise. "It's nice to see a familiar face!"

Oddly enough, she remembered the stiff derby, the celluloid collar and the buttoned shoes before she remembered the man and the eventful journey they'd once shared. "Mr. Folinsbee!" she said and smiled. "I didn't think we'd ever see you in Thunder Gulch again."

Bringing out his frilly handkerchief, he put it to use. "I'm on my way to Shoshone and then to Salt Lake," the drummer said. "Yonder freighter is taking me through, but he's not going over the Wolverine until morning. So I've got to stay here for the night, like it or not."

He shuddered. "I suppose it will have to be the Empire House again. It's as good as any, and that isn't saying much. I only hope I don't hear men talking of murder in the next room when I wake up tomorrow morning!"

Up until now she'd wanted to be rid of him. She was in no mood for small talk, and, after their first greeting, she'd scarcely been listening. But one word had driven into her consciousness as a pick drives into rock, and her hand darted out to his arm. "Murder!" she said. "What's this about murder?"

"I'm not saying there *was* a murder," he hastily amended. "I only know what I heard. My bed was up against the wall between my room and the one to the front of the building, and there was a knot hole in the wall. It had been plugged with paper, but the paper had fallen out. I couldn't help but hear what was being said in the next room, though the voices were faint at first, till the men began to get angry and excited. And that was when the one threatened to kill the other!"

She guessed that he'd told this tale many times, once he'd safely gotten out of Thunder Gulch, and that he took a macabre delight in retelling it. But she was in a frenzy of impatience to be done with this prelude and to get to the gist of his account.

"What did they say?" she demanded.

"One of them said, 'Did you think for a minute that I'd be interested in such a proposition? I've always known you were something of a rascal, but I never suspected you of being a fool! And there's only one thing for me to do. I'm going straight back to the girl and tell her the whole truth!'"

"And the other—?"

"He said, 'I had to gamble that you'd see it my way. But do you suppose I wasn't prepared to have you take this stand? Help me, and I'll make us both rich. Cross me, and I'll have to kill you!' The other one said, 'I don't think you've got the nerve!' Then I heard the door slam, and I knew that one of them had left the room. A minute or two after that, I heard the gun go off."

"A gun was fired from that room?" she demanded incredulously. "But I was sleeping in the hotel that morning, remember. I heard no shot."

"I didn't much more than hear it myself," Folinsbee said. "He must have wrapped his gun-hand in a blanket. That and the walls was enough to muffle the sound."

"Whose room was it?" she asked.

"I never learned. I got out of my room as fast as I could dress, and I never went back to the hotel. Calling on my trade that day—my line is fancy whiskies—I heard that a man named Hazzard was shot down in the street that morning, and I wondered if he were the one. I even thought of going to the law, but I was told the town had none. They were to elect a new marshal that afternoon. Frankly, Miss Kincaid, I was afraid to confess my knowledge. That night I found a freighter headed for Lewiston who was willing to take me along. But the whole matter has preyed on my conscience ever since, and if there's any law in this camp now, I intend to tell my story before I leave in the morning."

She was trembling violently, and she knew he was regarding her queerly. "I don't think that will be necessary," she managed to say.

Turning, she darted into the hotel, running up to the desk and flipping the pages of the register without a word to the astonished clerk. Coming at last to the page bearing the proper date, she ran her finger down to Ed Folinsbee's signature, noting the number of his room and the number of the room next to it to the front of the building—and the name of the man who'd occupied that room.

Then she was whisking up the stairs with a swish of her long skirts, and hurrying down the lighted hallway to that room where a man had made talk of murder. She drummed her knuckles upon the door, but no one made reply. Putting her hand to the knob, she found the door unlocked, so she opened it and stepped inside.

This room was rented; she could tell that at a glance. A man's clothes were strewn about and the bureau top held an assortment of personal belongings. But its occupant was gone, probably only for a moment since he'd left the door unlocked. A lamp burned dimly by the bedside, giving her light enough to cross to the window. She looked down into the street below, and she could see the spot which had been pointed out to her in days past—the spot where Jamieson Hazzard had fallen dead.

Thus she had finally gotten the proof that she needed, and she went back across the room, passing the bureau again and noticing a Colt forty-five that lay there. Picking it up, she found it loaded, and she held it tightly in her right hand, keeping it hidden in the folds of her dress as she left the room and came down the stairs.

Once onto the street, she faced to the west and hurried along, almost running yet keeping her pace from attracting the attention of others. In this manner she passed beyond the huddled buildings of the camp proper and came to the pathway leading up to Lars Thorson's house, and she hurried frantically then, groping along as she'd done last night when she'd fetched word that Rory O'Doone was for the taking. Reaching the shadowy porch, she beat upon the door with her left hand, gave it a shove and came into the hallway just as Dr. Drew appeared out of the living room.

"So they freed you!" he said. "I was beginning to fear that O'Doone didn't intend meeting our terms. Come in, my dear; come in! Did they harm you?"

"Doctor," she said, "don't you think it's about time to quit pretending?"

He was sidestepping back into the living room, and she came after him quickly, and she saw his face stiffen in the lamplight. "I'm not sure what you mean," he said slowly.

"It isn't the first time you've had trouble understanding me. When I refused the help that you and

Ginny and Tod Thorson offered me and went to work for Fee instead, you thought I'd gone over to the enemy. Jamieson Hazzard was dead, and you thought I was taking the easiest way to keep myself in comfort. That's the way it looked to you, wasn't it?''

Her voice had a hysterical edge to it, and he was looking at her in that same queer way Ed Folinsbee had regarded her. Backing to the fireplace, he said solicitously, "You're overwrought, Belle! Of course we've seen the truth by now. We understood when you came to us last night. You were stringing along with Fee and his bunch to get evidence against them. You wanted the man who killed Jamieson Hazzard."

"And I followed a long trail to find him," she said. "It never left the gulch, but it was a twisted, tangled trail. I've let myself be pawed by every ruffian in these diggings. I've danced with them and urged them to drink and talked to them when they were full of whiskey, trying to find out what I wanted to know. I'd have sold my soul for the answer—do you understand!—and considered it a good bargain! But the longest trail has an ending, and I've come to mine. And after I worked so hard to get the truth, I could laugh when I think how easily it finally came to me. Are you interested, Doctor?''

Drew's face was a study. "Go on," he said.

"No, I won't tell you about that," she decided. "There's a man in town who could stop a bullet before he has the chance to leave. I wouldn't want that to happen. I owe him more than I'll ever be able to pay, since he pointed the way to what I wanted to know. You killed Jamieson Hazzard, Doctor Drew."

He said, "You're mad—utterly mad!"

"Jamieson came to your hotel room that first morning, Doctor. You made him a proposition, but he wanted no part of it. He threatened to go to

Ginny and tell her some truth about you. You warned him, but he wasn't afraid! And after he'd left the room, you wrapped your gun-hand in a blanket and shot him down from your window!"

All the pretense left him then. "So now you know," he said.

"Yes," she said and, lifting the gun she'd taken from the room in the Empire House, she fired point-blank at him.

Yet in the very instant that she fired, she knew he'd been expecting her to, and she knew that she'd made a mistake in telling him so much and thereby forewarning him. He lurched sideways, her bullet driving a splinter from the fireplace mantel. She shifted the gun for a second and better shot, but his hand was darting under his coat, and the lamplight put a sheen on the weapon he produced. His bullet struck her hard and high, and she went down in a heap, fighting hard for consciousness and losing the fight . . .

Putting his smoking gun beneath his coat, Dr. Drew came cautiously across the room and stirred the unconscious figure with the tip of his toe. When Belle Kincaid didn't move, he reached and took the gun from her fingers, dropping it into his pocket. A spot of blood was growing above her left breast, the sight filling him with a wild panic. He thought, *"Steady! Steady, now!"* and was surprised that he'd said it aloud.

Moving toward the door, he went outside to the porch and stood listening for a long moment.

Satisfied that the sound of the shots had reached no one near enough to be interested, he came back into the living room and hoisted Belle Kincaid into his arms. Carrying her out of the house, he strode off across the shoulder of the slope for many paces, and at a spot where the shadows were thickest, he let her drop to the ground. He'd been careful to hold her in such a way as not to be soiled by her blood, and he returned to the house then and gave the living room his careful inspection.

The heavy acrid odor of powder smoke still clung to the air, so he hoisted a window. Next he kicked a small rug over a blood spot on the floor, felt in his pocket for a key and mounted the stairs to the second-story hallway. Pausing before a certain door, he inserted the key with his left hand, palming his gun with his right. The door swinging inward, he said, "Fee . . . ?"

This room had been a bedroom and the bed was still in it, but it had been stripped of anything that might have been converted into a rope. Matthew Fee lay stretched upon the bare springs. Coming to his feet at once, he crossed the room with quick strides, halting only when he saw the gun in Drew's hand. His coat off, Fee looked smaller, and he was certainly less florid. "What kind of cat-and-mouse game are you playing, vigilante?" he demanded. "I was to be hanged at sundown. That's long past. And what was the shooting downstairs a moment ago?"

"Never mind the shooting," Drew said. "Your hanging was postponed. Rory O'Doone ran off with Belle Kincaid and held her as a hostage. He made a deal to free her if we released you."

Hope flamed in Fee's eyes. "And he turned her loose?" he asked quickly.

Drew thought a moment before he answered. "The point is that I'm releasing you, Fee," he said. "And I've got something to say that you may find interesting. The miners are moving their gold out of the gulch tonight. There's a fortune heading toward Benton, Fee. A fortune for the taking."

Suspicion drew Fee's brows together. "Why are you telling me?"

"Because that treasure train could be taken over, Fee. All that's needed for the job is around fifty good men and a knowledge of the route the train is taking. You've got the men, or you can get them. I've got the knowledge that's needed. Are you interested in a partnership?"

"With *you?*"

Drew paused another moment. Then: "Didn't Rory O'Doone ever speak to you about me?" he asked. "Didn't he ever tell you an idea or two he had about me?"

Fee scowled and said, "I'm beginning to think that Rory strung along with me whenever it suited him and played a lone-wolf game whenever it suited him better. What about him?"

"You know he escaped the vigilantes last night. Do you suppose he could have done that if he hadn't been helped?"

Comprehension began to light Fee's eyes. "Are you trying to tell me *you* helped him get away?"

"Of course," Drew said. "And part of the bargain that I made with him was that he was to kill Tod Thorson the first chance he got. I'll say this for Rory, he made the try, but those damned Chinese took cards and spoiled the game. But of course you never heard about that. But have I convinced you that I've been doing a little lone-wolfing myself, and that we could do business tonight if we'd string along together?"

"I'm listening," Fee said. "I'm listening!"

Drew put his gun under his coat. "First we've got to get horses and start riding to wherever your men are hiding," he said. "We can do our talking on the trail."

Chapter Nineteen
BLACK WINGS FLUTTERING

Belle Kincaid, coming to consciousness, was first aware that she was very cold and very weary, and that the ground was hard beneath her and the night pressed thick and close. It wasn't until she tried moving that she remembered her hurt and came to a full realization of all that had happened to her. That was her worst moment. It was one thing to be so close to death that she could hear the black wings fluttering; it was another to know that she had had her chance at Jamieson Hazzard's murderer and failed, and that there'd never be a second chance.

After peering into the darkness for a long time, she recognized the black blob of the miner's court building and the looming bigness of Lars Thorson's house. It took a great deal of effort to pull her knees up beneath her, and she had a frantic moment when she found she hadn't the strength to come to her feet. Getting a hold on her underskirt, she managed to rip away a piece of it, and she folded the cloth into a crude pad and got it into place over her wound. She felt over the ground for her gun, not expecting to find it but just making sure, then she began crawling on hands and knees, heading toward the stone house.

She might have cried out, taking a chance that there'd be someone on this lonely slope to hear her, but she decided against it. She must spend her strength as a miser spends his pennies, reluctantly and with an eye to the greatest gain, so she held silent, crawling along until she saw the two men bulking in the darkness, coming down the trail from Lars Thorson's house. Huddling against the ground, she made ready to call to them, but one spoke, the other replied, and, recognizing both voices, she knew they were Matthew Fee and Dr. Drew. There'd be no help from either of them. Dr. Drew had removed her from the house, and Drew must have presumed her dead when he'd left her. Let him find her now, and he'd make very sure before he left her again.

The sight of that pair walking elbow to elbow, one as free as the other, hinted of an alliance with grim and awesome potentialities, and she was filled with a frantic need to reach someone and spread a warning. So she crawled onward, heading downhill now, her progress slow and painful. It was getting darker, she noticed, though that might have been her eyes playing her tricks. Last night there'd been a moon in the early evening, and even though the sky was overcast tonight, it should have been lighter than it was. She brushed her shoulder against a huge rock, not seeing it until it was too late, and that sent the pain flooding through her and she went unconscious again. Recovering, she found her bodice stiff with blood, and she hadn't the strength to put the crude bandage back into place.

She was lying sprawled when she heard footsteps again. Someone else was coming down the path from the direction of the stone house, this one moving on soft-soled feet and making very little sound. By the time she could see the approaching figure, she was afraid that the man was going to stumble over her. But he brought up short, pausing and staring down at her. Then, with a wild squawk of fear, he was gone, hurrying into the shadows.

That single cry had identified him for what he was, and she remembered that the Chinese were a nocturnal people. She could hear him padding away into the night, and she wondered if he'd come

back when he got the best of his fear, and she also
wondered if she'd be alive when he did return . . .

Tod Thorson had paced to the door of the *Trumpet*
office and peered out into the street so many times
that Ginny, seated at Hazzard's desk, finally said,
"Why don't you sit down, Tod? Either they free her
or they don't; and all you can do is wait and find out
which it will be. You're wearing a path in the floor!"

"The bargain was that they were to have her in
Thunder Gulch by an hour after sundown," Thorson
said. "The time limit is more than up."

"Maybe she's gotten back to camp and has gone
up to the stone house," Ginny suggested. "That's
vigilante headquarters, and Belle's first step would
be to report."

"Your father's up there," Thorson reflected.
"He'd send me word if she showed up."

That took his mind to Dr. Drew, and he was lost
in thought for a long time. Finally he came and
leaned against the desk. "Ginny, did your father get
a chance to talk to you today?" he asked.

"About his freeing Rory O'Doone last night, Tod?"
He nodded.

"Why, no," she said. "To tell you the truth, I've
scarcely seen him. This morning Quong Lee sent for
him, after the Chinese had carried you to Quong's
place. And this afternoon father was busy with Matthew Fee's trial, and I came here to work." She
paused, a nameless alarm in her eyes. "You told me
today, Tod, that he *did* let Rory go, and that he had a
good reason for doing it—a reason he'd explain to
me, himself. Why are you asking about him?"

"Just wondering," he said evasively and began
drumming his fingertips on the desktop. Then:
"Ginny, did you know that Absalom Wish was your
uncle?"

"Of course. Pi told me all about my family and its

background. Absalom was my mother's step-brother."

That jerked Thorson to alertness, but he hid any show of surprise by carefully building a smoke. "Stepbrother," he said casually. "You mean that Wish and your mother weren't blood relations?"

"Not at all. My mother's mother and Absalom Wish's father were each married twice. So you see, Wish wasn't really my mother's name, though she went by it till her own marriage. But why did you want to know? What difference does it make?"

Thorson, himself, was wondering what difference it made. He had detected a first flaw in the story Dr. Drew had told him at Quong Lee's that morning, but before he could find any real significance in the flaw or make any reply to Ginny's questions, the door heaved inward and a Chinaman darted into the office. Small and of indefinite age, he looked like a hundred others Thorson had seen around the diggings. "Quong Lee say you comee quick!" he cried. "Hully now!"

His tone was so urgent that Thorson didn't pause for questions. Grasping Ginny's hand, he said, "Come along!" Out of the *Trumpet* building, they hurried along, Thorson keeping his eye on the bobbing pigtail of the Chinese as the man led them along the street toward the western end of the gulch, finally coming to the turn that brought them to the Chinese diggings. Here the huddled warrens of Quong Lee's people rose against the night, and the house of Quong Lee was aglow with lanterns, a swarm of Chinese milling before the open door. They parted to make a pathway for the three who came hurrying up, and Thorson shouldered into Quong Lee's shack and instantly saw who lay in the bed he'd occupied not many hours before.

He'd waited for Belle Kincaid's return; now she was here, but this was not the way he'd wanted to

see her. For he knew at once that she was dying.
Ginny cried, "Belle! Belle!", her heart in her voice.

Quong Lee made a high, round-shouldered figure
against the wall, his face many-hued in the light of
the multicolored lanterns. "Like last night, I order
my people to be eyes and ears for vigilantes
throughout gulch," he said. "This is what one
found. My poor skill is not sufficient to recover bullet."

"Then she's—?"

Quong nodded solemnly. "She has called your
name constantly. Humbly suggest you learn what is
to be learned at once."

Coming closer to the bed, Thorson dropped down
beside it. One of Belle's hands lay white and still
against the cover, and he took it into his own hand
and said softly, "Belle. I'm here. This is Tod Thorson."

She looked so pale that at first he thought he'd
come too late, yet there was a feeble pulse in the
wrist beneath his fingers and after a while her eye-
lids fluttered open and she looked at him as though
she found it hard to see. Ginny sobbed, the sound
breaking the hush holding the room. "Ginny?"
Belle said. "She's here?"

"Yes," Thorson said. "Belle, who did this to you?"

"Lean closer," she said. "It's hard to raise my
voice."

He put his ear above her lips, but for a while she
said nothing, her hand clenching spasmodically in
his. Then she whispered, "I've got to tell you the
truth, Tod. But don't let Ginny know—ever. I found
him tonight, the man who killed Jamieson . . .
Doctor Drew . . ."

It was his hand that tightened this time, and he
turned cold all over. "You're sure?" he said.

"Remember Ed Folinsbee, the drummer . . . on
the stage? He's back in Thunder Gulch. He heard

Drew and Jamieson arguing . . . in the hotel room
. . . that first morning. Drew threatened Jamieson,
shot him from the window. I came to the stone
house tonight . . . faced him with the truth . . .
tried to shoot him. He shot me instead. Now he's
freed Matthew Fee . . . They came out of the house
together . . ."

That last was as startling a piece of news as the
first she gave him, but he held silent, straining to
hear all of her speech. "I went to the stone house
with one thought, and one alone," she whispered
clearly. "Since then I've had time for thinking. But I
can't be sure . . . Ginny's happiness would mean a
lot to Jamieson . . . I know that . . . Do you understand what I'm trying to say, Tod?"

"I think I do," he said, low-voiced. "But he's got
to answer for this."

"She'll need you . . . need you as she's never
needed anyone before. Remember that and—
ah-h . . ."

This wasn't the first time he had ever seen a person die, yet her passing filled him with a baffling
sense of impotency, for it seemed so wrong that she
should slip beyond his reach and his help while he
was still holding fast to her. When he came to his
feet, Ginny said, "Tod, your eyes are wet! Then she's
—she's—?"

He nodded. "The kindest way to put it is to say
that she and Jamieson Hazzard have joined each
other at last."

Drawing the blanket over Belle Kincaid's face, he
turned to see Ginny's shoulders trembling. Putting
his arms around her, he let her do her weeping
against him. But he had a need for every precious,
fleeting minute, and at last he spoke over her head
to Quong. "I haven't time to tell you everything she
told me," Tod said. "Matthew Fee has gotten free,
Quong."

The Chinese nodded. "Same is known to me. One of my people witnessed his hasty departure from stone house and made report."

There was no reading a blind man's eyes, but Thorson knew that Quong Lee was aware that Dr. Drew had left with Fee, and he also knew that Quong Lee, understanding part of the situation, would keep the truth from Ginny. He said, "I've got to ride after the treasure train, Quong. I'll be grateful if you'll look after Ginny and—" He nodded toward the bed.

Again Quong Lee nodded, and Thorson led Ginny outside, the clustering Chinese making a path for them once more, and when he'd taken her a distance he put his finger under her chin, tilting it and finding the strength to meet her hazel eyes.

"Ginny, before I ride, I want to ask you something," he said. "Will you marry me? Tomorrow?"

She met his gaze, but not his question. "Who killed her, Tod?" she asked. "She found the man she was looking for, didn't she—the one who killed Pi. Who was he?"

Feeling naked before her searching gaze, he held his own eyes steady, toying with the notion of telling her the truth lest she discover it in crueler fashion later. But there was that dying wish of Belle's to remember. "Rory O'Doone was the man," he said. "He brought her to the stone house, swapped her for Fee and pretended to leave. Your father set out to catch up with the treasure train, and Belle started for her own cabin. Rory shot her on the way, left her for dead, and the Chinese found her. Rory was afraid of her, you see. On the way into Thunder Gulch, he'd confessed to her that he was the man she was hunting."

She was silent for a moment, and he wondered how much her intuition had told her and how much of his story she would believe. Looking up at him she said, "You asked me a question, Tod. The answer's yes. I'll be proud to marry you."

She raised her lips and he kissed her, feeling her arms tightening about him, and he clung to her for a long, long time. "I've got to be riding, darling," he finally said. "You know that. Everything's at stake, now. Promise me you'll stay with Quong Lee till I get back."

She nodded, her eyes all shining, and this leaving her was the hardest thing he had ever done. Fifteen minutes later found him up on a livery stable horse and heading out across the desolate flats toward the Old South Road. . . .

By the time a hidden trail had brought Matthew Fee and Dr. Drew to the base of the sheer precipice and Fee had sought out a certain boulder and the rift behind it, the two of them had done a great deal of talking. Now Drew hauled on the reins of the saddler he'd taken from a Thunder Gulch hitchrail and said, "Once beyond this cliff, the situation is reversed, eh, Fee? I'm the fly and you're the spider, then. You still don't know the route the treasure train is taking. But you could find a way to get that information cheaply—just as you found out where Eph Tutt kept his gold hidden."

Fee put a frowning speculation upon this remark before he grinned. "We seem to have gotten to the fork of the trail where we have to trust each other," he said. "You know the secret of Michigan Hole right now, and you'd be a dead man if I didn't think you could keep it. No, Doc, I won't torture you to find out about that treasure train. And I'll see that your share from the raid is as big as my share, just like we agreed on the way out here. I made Tod Thorson a proposition once. I told him I wasn't out to hog all the gold that was to be had, and I said that those who strung along with me got treated right.

He turned that proposition down. But it's still my stand, Drew."

It was a time for desperate gambling and long chances, and Dr. Drew took his. Reaching into his pocket for the gun he'd gotten from Belle Kincaid, he extended the weapon to Fee. Then he drew his muffler up about his face, masking himself to the eyes. "No need to mention my name to your boys," he said. "There might be hotheads with itchy fingers who'll remember that I ordered three of them hanged last night. Besides that, I'd like to leave the way clear to become an honest man again, once this night's work is over. The less people who know the truth, the better. Do you follow me?"

"I'm half a horse ahead of you." Fee chuckled. "This might just be a starter. What a pair of partners we're going to make, Doc!"

Then Fee was leading the way through the rift in the rock, and the great grass-carpeted bowl spread before them, pale and ethereal with a ghost of a moon above, just fighting free of a cloudy prison. They rode toward the scattering of cabins under the second cliff, a score of men coming to meet them, Rory O'Doone at their head.

"Boss!" Rory cried exultantly. "So they turned you loose!"

Fee reined short. "Yes," he said, cold as death, "they turned me loose, Rory. But they wouldn't have got me in the first place if you hadn't had a mile-wide yellow streak that loosened your big mouth. Do you know what happens to men who double-cross me, Rory?"

O'Doone took half a step backward. "I had to talk, boss!" he said. "It was either talk or have my neck stretched! And I made it up to you! I got the Kincaid woman and sent a note, offering to swap her for you. That's why they turned you loose. *Matt —NO—!*"

Moonlight put a sheen on the gun that came into Matthew Fee's hand, and Rory O'Doone, seeing that dancing light, might have had the time to make his play if he'd only tried. Instead he went down on his knees, his broad face contorted with a hideous fear, and he was that way, his arms half-raised as though to ward off death as it came. Dust spurted over his left shirt pocket, the cliffs caught the thunder of Fee's gun, hurling it from one wall to another, and Rory O'Doone went over backwards to sprawl grotesquely.

Blowing smoke from the gun-barrel, Fee held the weapon, his eyes running over the gathered men who were now nearly a full fifty, and he looked to see if any one of them wanted to play out a dead man's hand. "That probably looked mighty sudden to you boys," he said. "But I've just made this hideout a safer place for all of us. If anybody thinks I was too hasty, just think that over. Now get gear onto your cayuses and get ready to ride."

At Fee's elbow, Drew leaned and whispered. "The Old South Road," he said. "They figured that no one would suspect them of heading that way."

Fee raised his brows, a man quick to appreciate another's strategy. "The Old South Road," he announced to his men. "A treasure train's rolling along it, packing all the gold of the diggings. You'll be rich by morning, boys, and you'll never have to fear a vigilante rope. This is the showdown, and the winners take everything!"

Chapter Twenty
SOUTH ROAD SHOWDOWN

Earlier that evening, Pat Shea had counted nearly thirty noses in the gathering darkness of the canyon down the Old South Road, and when he'd threaded his way among the vigilantes to the last of the looming wagons and huddled saddle horses, he said, "Looks like everybody's here that's coming. But how about the Chinks? Ain't they sending their gold out?"

Josh Hoskins had his stagecoach at the tag end of the cavalcade. "I'm packing their dust for 'em," he announced. "Don't you reckon we'd better be rolling, Pat?"

Shea said, "I guess so. Everything seems to be in order, but I'm jumpy as a cat tonight."

They had twenty vehicles in all; some were high-sided ore wagons, a few tandem-hitched with six span of horses to pull them, and some were lighter wagons, carrying dust. The word going along the line, those who were to drive climbed to their perches, the others hauled themselves into saddles and strung out along either side of the wagons, and in this manner they made themselves ready for the starting signal. Shea put himself up on the first wagon, the crack of his whip sending the horses against their harness, and the trek was on.

They had hard going from the very first, the same rough sort of passage Thorson had found when he'd tooled Matthew Fee's stolen wagon along this same trail. A walking man could have paced them with time to spare, and even when they'd skirted the worst of the rocky outcroppings and the going smoothed out after the first few miles, they had their troubles. A flirtatious moon, alternately showing its face and hiding it, was of little help. They passed the charred ruin of the road agent shebang they'd burned the previous night and came to where the canyon walls pinched together, and here a small landslide blocked the way. Josh Hoskins, who'd run his stage over this road in the earlier days before the Wolverine Pass route was put through, had anticipated this sort of emergency. It was at his suggestion that shovels had been fetched along.

"Out and dig!" Shea ordered, and the word went down the line.

They were at the task and had it almost finished when Thorson overtook them, the ring of his horse's hoofs against rock bringing a display of artillery into sudden evidence. He came up the line to Shea's wagon, and when the shovels were stowed away and the treasure train moved onward, he paced Shea, the two of them making their talk above the rumble of the wagon.

"I saw the Kincaid woman just before I cleared camp," Shea said. "I suppose you turned Fee loose, once she showed herself. Any chance that he knows what's up?"

More than a score of lives were at stake here. Thorson had thought of that as he'd ridden to overhaul the train, and it made guilty knowledge out of the secret he wanted to keep for Ginny's sake. "Fee's loose, Pat," he admitted. "And I'm afraid there's a good chance that he knows what we're doing. I'm going on guesswork, but I've reason to think my guess is good. I'll pass the word along the train for the boys to keep their eyes peeled."

He made a quick turn down the line and back again, and rifles that had been stowed in sheaths were balanced across saddle horns when he rode alongside Shea again. He was afraid the big Celt might press him for details about Fee, but Shea was kept busy at his work, and there was silence between them. And thus it went, the wagons rumbling along, jolting and bouncing, the harness creaking, the voices of the drivers drifting low and urgent whenever the way was rough. Thunder Gulch was moving its gold, and the men who rode with it were ready for whatever the night might bring.

The canyon behind them, they came out into a grassy valley, made narrow by the shouldering hills that pressed closely on either side. Moonlight silvered the low clumps of bushes and made ghostly sentinels out of the scattered trees. Here the cavalcade had the easiest going of the trip, but it was here that Thorson began to feel a jumpy nervousness, and his quick glances to the left and right were more frequent, his restlessness becoming so acute that he tried to laugh it away. He did not know of Michigan Hole, and there were none to tell him that the road agent hideout was almost directly to the west and that there were trails to bring riders to this grassy valley. He only had intuition to serve him, but when the first rifle spoke, it was almost as though he'd expected the attack.

But that was only the beginning.

Fifty yards above, on the slope of the hill to his left, a rifle spun a red blossom against the night. Marking the flash, Thorson brought his gun arcing up, triggering at that brief brightness. From the corner of his eye he could see the driver who tooled a pair of tandem-hitched ore wagons directly behind Shea. The man was standing up as though for a good look. Slowly bowing at the waist, the fellow pitched face forward off the wagon, the wheel horses kicking in sudden frenzy.

Then rifles were speaking everywhere, and sixshooters too, a half a hundred guns divided between one hillside and the other, catching the treasure train in a withering crossfire. Somebody was shouting, *"Road agents! Road agents!"* Horses squealed frantically, vigilante guns made puny reply to the ambushed attackers, and above all this bedlam, Pat Shea tried to make his orders heard. "Under the wagons!" he bellowed over and over again. "Get to cover under the wagons!"

Once the first paralyzing moment of surprise was over, they were quick to obey him. Men came tumbling down from their exposed perches, those with cooler heads jerking the brake levers to the last ratchets before dismounting. Thus, on a level stretch like this, the horses could only rear and pitch, unable to haul away the heavy ore wagons in their fright. But the drivers with lighter vehicles were having trouble. Thorson, thundering down the line to pass Shea's order along, found Josh Hoskins calmly unharnessing his team, thus making sure that one cargo of dust wasn't going to be carried off into road agent hands. Seeing Hoskins' idea, Thorson lent help with fractious horses wherever he could.

Meanwhile the mounted vigilantes were stationing themselves beneath wagons, their guns banging at either slope, and Thorson could hear the high-pitched whine of bullets as the battle raged. Off his horse, he stumbled toward the shelter of a wagon and almost pitched headlong over a fallen man. It was Cory, and his voice was thick with pain as he said, "They had one with my name on it . . . !"

Thorson found a rifle beside the vigilante, and he picked it up and put it to his shoulder just as Cory died. Likely there'd be many dead before this night was through.

Pat Shea came crawling along, checking on his men, and Thorson said, "What do you make of it, Pat?" Then, marking a gun-flash, he sent three quick shots in its direction. A man screamed stridently, straightened from behind a bush near the top of the hill and was starkly silhouetted for a moment, his hands upflung, before he tumbled downward. "What do I make of it?" Shea said. "It's shaping up to be massacre, Tod! They've got us outnumbered, if I'm any judge, and they've got us where they want us. They picked the time and the place, damn 'em!"

He went on about his business, and Thorson put all his concentration on the task of making his bullets count. By the time Cory's rifle grew hot, the road agents had worked down either slope and were hunkered in the bushes fringing the bottom of the hills, within easy six-gun range. Thorson could see their whole strategy then: to close in from either side, whittling down the odds as they inched forward and making their task the easier when the time came for a last, finishing rush.

"How soon do you think they'll try it?" a gentle voice asked, and Thorson found that Zeke Lockhart had come crawling up beside him. The rifles on the slopes cut loose in a sharp, racketing fury, and Thorson waited for the end of that barrage before he said, "Soon, I'd guess. I've been thinking, Zeke. We've been hours on the trail but, considering our pace, we're not so many miles out of Thunder Gulch. If I could Injun through them and back to camp, I ought to be able to round up enough miners to make a difference in this man's fight. We won a lot of them over when we put Matt Fee on trial."

"You'd never get past them, Tod," Lockhart said. "They'll be counting on us trying for help."

The moon went edging into a cloudbank, a shadow slid across the valley, and the rifles fell silent for a moment. Matthew Fee's voice came booming out of the hush. "It's your gold we want, not your scalps!" he shouted. "Throw down your guns and we'll call it off!"

Pat Shea, somewhere up the line, made answer

for all of them. "To hell with you, Fee. You'd never let a man of us live to see Thunder Gulch again. You wouldn't dare. Not now!"

Fee laughed, the rising clatter of guns drowning out the sound, but Thorson thought he'd located the direction from which the taunting voice had come. "Zeke?" he said. "You still here? I've got to try it before the moon shows again. Tell Pat, if you see him."

Then he came out from under the wagon on his hands and knees and went forward in this manner for a dozen yards, flattening as the air-lash of a bullet fanned his cheek. He'd almost been killed by one of the vigilantes, and he wished there'd been time to pass the word that he'd be out here. Waiting, he felt the perspiration along his back, and his face was wet and sticky with it. He tore the bandage from his head, conscious that it made a good, glimmering target in the darkness, wormed forward another few yards, saw a clump of bushes ahead and reached it by a sudden wild lunge. A man cursed in his astonishment, a gun banged almost in Thorson's face and he felt the tug of lead along his sleeve. He sent his right fist smashing forward in the darkness and felt his knuckles connect with something solid. The man down, Thorson was on top of him, hitting hard and frantically.

The road agent went still and Thorson couldn't tell whether he'd killed him or knocked him unconscious, and it didn't much matter. He made for the slope again, reached it and began angling upward, clawing from one clump of bushes to another. A burst of rifle fire toward the north told him that road agents had been strung out to keep anyone from turning back along the road toward the canyon. Over the hill was the only way out, and it was from this direction that Fee's voice had come. Stooping low, Thorson climbed as quickly as he could, fighting his way through the thicker brush and stumbling over deadfall logs. A glance at the sky told him there'd be moonlight mighty soon, and when it came he saw two men not far above him, standing near the crest of this low hill. It was too late to get to cover.

Laughing, Matthew Fee said, "So it's Thorson! I would have bet that you'd be making some such damn' fool try as this!"

Thorson started his gun tilting upward. "And it's you and me and the finish, Fee!" he said.

Thus these two, archenemies from the first time they'd laid eyes on each other, stood now face to face, and for the last time. Only one of them would walk away from this meeting. Thorson could see a gun in Fee's hand, but he put his eyes on that diamond solitaire in Fee's shirtfront, and his thought was that it made a fine target at a time like this. He knew he was matching Fee's gun-speed, but he also knew it would be touch and go between them, the thought passing through his mind in less time than a watch takes to tick. Then the sledging slam of a bullet hit him high and hard in his left shoulder, almost catapulting him down the slope. As he went over backwards, he realized that it hadn't been Fee who'd fired, but the other man, the tall one with the muffler wrapped about his face—Dr. Drew.

Coming up against a bush, Thorson rolled, propped up on one elbow and got in a shot. It was aimed at Drew, and there wasn't time to weigh the rights or wrongs of it, or to think of Ginny—not when it was a matter of shoot or be shot. Stiffening, Drew clutched at his own shoulder, his gun falling from his fingers. Before Thorson could get in another shot, the man wheeled, darting into a clump of bushes. Fee said, "He's had his turn; I'm still waiting mine. I wanted it to be fair between us,

Thorson, to get the taste of last night's licking out of my mouth."

Fee's gun boomed then, the lead geysering dust into Thorson's face, and Tod rolled again, heedless of his wounds, and firing as he rolled. It was a snapshot; there wasn't time for anything better, and he wasn't sure where it went. He fired once more and Fee seemed to lose girth and stature. Taking two teetering steps forward, the man drew in his breath and let it out again and fell across Thorson's fee. "See you in hell, Thorson," he said—and died.

Thorson got to his feet. That took an effort, but he made it, for he had a desperate need to get into those bushes and search out Dr. Drew, a need that had become more important than running the road agent gantlet and getting out of the valley. There was a wild stirring in the bushes, and his first thought was that Drew was coming back after him, but a dozen road agents bulked in the moonlight and were upon him, bearing him down beneath their weight.

At least these men couldn't use their guns, not working at such close quarters as this, but the fight Thorson put up was feeble, the pain in his shoulder taking the strength out of him. *This is the finish*, he thought, and that was when the road agents scattered, piling off him and darting frantically for the cover of the bushes. He couldn't understand that sudden retreat, the night swam hazily before his eyes and was filled with multiple figures that came swarming down the slope with a great deal of banging of guns.

Then he did understand. These were Quong Lee's Chinese, a half a hundred of them working down the slope, and he tried to thrill to the implication of their presence, but the spirit wasn't in him. They were everywhere; some had guns, some knives, some only clubs, but all of them had a savage fury, and to Thorson it seemed the most sensible thing to crawl over to a bush, put his back to it and just watch. The rifles below, gone silent for a moment, began banging again. Somebody was shouting in a high, shrill voice, *"The Chinks! The Chinks! They're on both slopes! Come on, boys. Now we've got the road agents in a crossfire!"*

Thorson smiled a tired smile and let himself slip into unconsciousness then. When he opened his eyes, Shea and Lockhart and others, come to beat the last of the road agents out of the brush, were lifting him to a stand. They got him down to the wagons and made a bandage for his wound, and he said, "Just patch me up so I can sit a saddle, and it will do. I'm heading back to Thunder Gulch as quick as I can. I don't think this train is going to have any more trouble. Once I get back to camp, I'll have Quong Lee take a look at my hurt. Or is he here?"

"No, Quong didn't come along," Lockhart told him. "The Old South Road is no place for a blind man to try walking. But Quong must have guessed that we were going to have trouble. These boys of his tell us that Quong ordered them to arm themselves and to tail us toward Shoshone, and I'm mighty glad he did. Also I'm glad that you had the idea of including the Chinese in the vigilantes, Tod. Between the bunch of us we've broken the back of the road agent outfit tonight. We found Matt Fee on the hillside near you—dead. And we've got other men to bury—theirs and ours. Cory got it, so did Mulligan and Marks and one of the boys from Tom Conway's old crew. Josh Hoskins was nicked, and so were some of the others, but they swear it's nothing that a squirt of tobacco juice, a stiff drink and a neckerchief bandage won't fix. We've got quite a few prisoners. Do you feel up to holding trial right here by the road?"

They came threading among the milling vigilantes, white and yellow, to where a score of men stood sullenly beneath the watchful guns of guards. Thorson looked the prisoners over, seeing a few faces he recognized—Sooner Dobbs' and Joe Coulter's and Jake DeSpain's—and many that he didn't know, but the high figure of Dr. Drew was not among them. And looking at these men, Thorson was suddenly tired of hangings and violence and bloodshed, and he said, "Zeke, we're executive officers of the vigilantes, and it's up to us to decide. Cory and others died tonight, but they left dead behind too. Maybe that balances up. I say rope these fellows together and walk 'em on into Shoshone with the train. Once you get 'em there, see that they scatter and keep going. I'll bet that we'll never see any of them again."

"Probably you're right," Lockhart agreed. "Vigilante work is finished. But what about the Hurdy-Gurdy House? Will you put a torch to it when you get back to the gulch?"

Thorson remembered another fire, the one in the *Trumpet* building, and he remembered the hurdy-gurdies who'd toiled in the bucket brigade. "There's nothing wrong with the Hurdy-Gurdy House that won't be made right now that Fee is dead," he said. "Our job in Thunder Gulch from here on out will be to build, not to burn, Zeke."

And so it was decided, and when the burying was done in the last of the moonlight, Thorson stepped up into his saddle, and the Chinese, their work finished, prepared to go back to Thunder Gulch with him. Lifting his hand in a farewell salute to the treasure train, Thorson jogged his horse and headed north, the Chinese trotting briskly behind him, making a bedlam of talk.

His shoulder throbbed, but the pain wasn't too great, and his pace was far too slow to suit him. His greatest sickness came with the thought that Drew had escaped. He hadn't dared ask Shea or Lockhart or others if Drew had been among the road agent dead, but he had his answer anyway, for if Drew's body had been found, the word would have reached him. Thus there was this one last piece of vigilante work left unfinished, and it presented the devil's own dilemma.

When they came into the canyon, he reined short and said, "I'm riding on ahead, boys." The Chinese began their chattering again, and he couldn't tell whether they'd understood him. He said, "You're a good bunch of boys—a damned good bunch of boys."

Most of the night was gone when he came again to Thunder Gulch, and he headed first for Quong Lee's, knowing that the Chinese would want a report of all that had happened, and mindful of his wound besides, and of the skill the man could put to mending it. When he got beyond the town proper and to the Chinese diggings, he saw that light still glowed in Quong Lee's shack. The man himself stood in the open doorway, making a high silhouette, and he bowed gravely as Thorson came down off his horse.

"Is Thorson?" Quong asked. "Quick return indicates troubles mostly gone like mists before morning sunshine."

"Thanks to you and your people," Thorson said, and by then he was at the doorway and had his look inside. He could see the bed where Belle Kincaid had died, and another was in it, a gaunt man with a bandaged shoulder—Dr. Drew. But it was not at him that Tod Thorson really looked, but at Ginny Drew, who sat beside the bed. To Thorson that made it a worse moment than any the night had brought, for he could tell from the look of her that now she knew all the hideous truth.

Chapter Twenty-one
EYES THAT SAW NOT

Thorson took a step into the room, the thin scrape of his boot sole and the shallow breathing of Dr. Drew the only sounds to break the deathly hush. Meeting the brittle stare of the man in the bed, he looked at Ginny again. "So he came here!" Thorson said. "He needed a doctor and there is only one in Thunder Gulch. Ginny, I hope—"

"I've stayed here since you left," Ginny said tonelessly. "I was in the next room when he came a short while ago, wild-eyed and bloody and demanding that Quong Lee take care of his wound. He fainted while Quong was working on him, and he's just recovered. But he doesn't need to say any more; I've heard enough. Tod, you kept the truth from me, didn't you?"

But Thorson made no answer for suddenly he was seeing the ghost of a hope and the ghost of a truth and the way to make them tangible. Stepping toward the bed, he flung back the blanket covering Drew. The man lay naked from the waist up except for the bandage Quong Lee had put over the shoulder wound that Thorson's bullet had made. "Yes, Ginny, I lied to you," Thorson admitted. "But I didn't guess the whole truth myself until this moment. I had a lot of time for thinking while I was riding back to camp, and now I've got the proof. Belle had time for thinking while she lay dying, and she glimpsed the truth, too, but she couldn't be sure. From what she and this man said to each other on the stage the day we came to camp, I gathered that they'd never actually met in the California days.

That's why Belle was fooled. Quong, will you come here?''

"Not necessary," Quong said. "These eyes too dim for seeing, but fingers tell much when exploring for bullet. Is good.''

Ginny's eyes were puzzled. "I—I don't understand," she said.

"Is brave legend in California," Quong explained. "Perhaps you have heard deathless tale of encounter between Dr. Drew and Lars Thorson and fierce mountain lion. Man mauled by angry cat carries scars to grave. Yet this person on bed has no scars. Conclusion is obvious.''

"Don't you see?" Thorson cried. "He's *not* Huntley Drew! He can't be. Lars Thorson was scarred badly, and so was your father!''

"Then he's—he's an impostor! But who is he, Tod?''

There was only one answer, and Thorson had it now. "Dr. Absalom Wish.''

The man on the bed gave them a cold and hateful look. "Do all of you have to stand here with your mouths hanging open?" he demanded. "This shoulder's on fire. Quong, can't you do something for me?''

Kneeling beside a low teak table, Quong Lee fingered an array of bottles and poured a potion from one of them. "Here is medicine made from nameless herb," he said. "Good for numbing pain. But this poor physician requires fee in return—*the truth!*''

The man on the bed said, "I was a fool to have come to you, you slant-eyed devil. You guessed more than half the truth from the first, and you've waited for a chance like this, damn you. The minute I walked in here tonight, I knew there was no use pretending that I'd got this wound from a road agent's gun. I should have let myself bleed to death on the trail!"

"Not too late to allow you to do so," Quong said meaningly.

"Give me your medicine. Hanging will be easier than the way you'd like to see me die! I'll answer all the questions you've got to ask."

Quong spooned the medicine into him; his patient gagged and part of the potion dribbled into his Imperial. Thorson said, "The first thing we want to know is this: what did you do with Huntley Drew?"

"He's buried in Yucatán. While I was down with fever, he got the truth out of me about that Sierraville raid in the old days. You know about that, since you read his diary. When my fever broke, I had a faint memory of talking in my delirium. I faced him up with it, and he admitted that he knew everything. That was too much for him to know, and I saw that he never got back to the States with his knowledge. I brought all his papers back with me, but I reported the death of Absalom Wish instead of Huntley Drew. Because I'd decided to become him after I reached San Francisco."

"Why, Wish?"

"Because I found a letter waiting for him in Frisco—a letter from Jamieson Hazzard, here in Thunder Gulch, explaining that Drew and you, Thorson, were the heirs to Lars Thorson's rich discovery claim. It was a fortune for the taking, and I reasoned that I could pass myself off as Drew easily enough in an out-of-the-way frontier camp. Not many people knew either of us well, seeing as we'd spent most of our lives in the forgotten corners. We were about the same build, and I grew an Imperial like his, reasoning that that would make me enough like him to fool any Californians who might be in Thunder Gulch and who might have seen the pair of us in the old days."

Thorson showed his surprise. "Did you think that would fool Hazzard?"

"No, Hazzard was my real stumbling block. But I hoped I could buy him. Hazzard started out to amount to something in life, but he'd ended up by running a down-at-the-heels newspaper in a backwoods camp. Lean living kicks the ideals out of a lot of men, and I thought that a cut of the gold from the discovery claim might make a good Indian out of him. All I wanted was a chance to talk to him before he started crying, 'Impostor!' I expected a bad time at the Thunder Gulch stage depot when the wrong man climbed off the stage, so I pretended an attack of neuralgia as an excuse to keep my face covered. That way, Hazzard wouldn't have had a real look at me till we were off alone somewhere. As it was, he failed to meet the stage, so we never saw each other till he came to my room next morning."

"And then you must have tried to buy his silence," Thorson said. "You made your proposition, but Hazzard hadn't changed in all these years. He probably denounced you, so you shot him from the hotel window after he left. Ed Folinsbee, the whiskey drummer, had the next hotel room, and he heard the two of you arguing. He told Belle about it last night, and she told me before she died. From that moment on, I knew that you'd killed Hazzard, even though it made no sense to me. Huntley Drew was Hazzard's friend. That's what started me thinking along the track that brought me to the truth."

Ginny said, "Now I know why you lied to me, Tod, and blamed Rory O'Doone for what happened to Belle."

A spasm of pain shook Wish, and Quong Lee was quick to give him more medicine. "That story you told me about Rory O'Doone was partly the truth," Thorson said. "But I want the straight of it now."

"O'Doone was in the California diggings, just as I

told you, and he was one of the men who rode with me on that Sierraville raid. When he saw me at the miner's court election that first afternoon, he thought he recognized me. So he had a look through my luggage, hoping to find something to give him proof that I was Wish instead of Drew, and even though it was Drew's luggage, that diary gave him a glimmering of the truth. That was my big mistake, ever keeping the diary, but up until then I'd thought I was safe enough.

"Rory faced me with his suspicions quite a while ago. He came to the stone house several times when you two were at the *Trumpet* office. At first I kept his big mouth closed by paying him a little money, and later by giving him information that put dust in his pockets. I'm the one who advised him to keep an eye on Frenchy Thiebault, and I also let him know that Eph Tutt had gold worth getting. Rory shared some of that information with Matt Fee and other road agents, but he never let them know the truth about me. Rory was the man to see the sense in keeping a good game to himself, but he paid for his lone-wolfing when he double-crossed Fee. Fee shot him last night, just before the road agents took the trail after the treasure train."

"So you were the spy in the vigilantes!" Thorson said.

"And I let Rory escape—but not to protect the dubious reputation of Absalom Wish. I had a chance then to get rid of Rory and his blackmailing, but even though I thought he was bluffing about having written down what he knew and passing the paper to a friend, I couldn't be sure. I turned him loose, and part of the bargain was that he was to kill you, Thorson. There'd be twice as much gold if I owned the discovery claim alone, but by that time I was playing for even bigger stakes—the gold shipment that would someday go out of Thunder Gulch. When the chance came last night to make a try for that, I had to throw in with Fee."

"But why did you tell me part of the truth about Rory?" Thorson asked. "If I hadn't wanted to believe in you, for Ginny's sake, I might have smelled out the whole truth then."

"When I'd gone to bed, the other night after the vigilante hangings, I heard Ginny come out of your room. Later I heard you rummaging in the trunk, and then you left the stone house. I'd been pretending to be asleep. I got up and had a look in the trunk, and the diary wasn't exactly where I'd left it. I didn't know how much you knew or had guessed, but I was fairly certain that Ginny had told you what she must have suspected about Rory and myself. What easier way to disarm you than admit the very thing you'd expect me to want secret?"

"And those four names on the back of the envelope—Lars' and Hazzard's and Quong Lee's and O'Doone's?"

"They were written just as I told you, one night after Rory went through the luggage. Only I didn't write them because they were the men who might have known about that Sierraville raid. No, they were the men of Thunder Gulch who could have exposed me as an impostor. Thorson and Hazzard's names were crossed out because they were dead, and consequently no menace. Neither was Quong, for how could a blind man see through my masquerade? Rory O'Doone was the question mark then. I soon learned how I stood with him!"

"So that's it!" Thorson said. "And I was a fool not to have guessed all along, but I suppose a man's always blind to what he doesn't want to see. Even when Hazzard lay dead in the *Trumpet* office, your only thought was to go and have a look at the discovery claim. And the night after Fee fired the *Trumpet* building, you tried to talk me into leaving Thunder Gulch and letting you handle the discovery claim all by your lonesome. It's the gold you were after from the first. And you're the man we made head of the vigilantes! Zeke Lockhart and I agreed last night that we were through with hangings. But even if I were Lars Thorson, himself, I don't think I'd be able to stop what will happen when the vigilantes return and the whole truth comes out!"

Wish signaled for more medicine, and as Quong Lee began spooning it, Wish said, "I'd have won! I'd have beaten all of you if you hadn't had the devil's own luck, Thorson. It's wrong, wrong, that all of you high-minded fools—Lars Thorson, Hazzard, Belle, Quong, Huntley Drew, Ginny and you—should have won out over me in the end!"

He sank back exhausted against a silken pillow, and Tod reached and took Ginny's hand, feeling the coldness of it, and it was a long time before he realized that Wish's shallow breathing had ceased and that the man was dead. Quong Lee felt for the man's pulse, drew the blanket over his face, padded to the doorway and clapped his hands. There were half a dozen alpaca-clad men who came to carry Absalom Wish from the room, and after they were gone Quong said, "Is blood on your shoulder, friend. Weary physician gets no rest."

"I'd almost forgotten," Tod said.

While Quong Lee worked at extracting the bullet, Thorson set his teeth together and it was mighty bad for a while. Ginny, finding herself in the way of the men, wandered out of the shack, and Thorson waited until she was gone before he said, "Quong, I know that your people must have reported to you that Drew, or Wish rather, left with Matthew Fee last night. You guessed what they were going to do, so you sent your men to help protect the treasure train. I understand all of that. But there's something else I'm wondering about, something I couldn't help but notice. You fed Wish medicine until his story was told, but the last dose you gave him came from a different bottle over there on the table."

There was no reading the blankness of Quong Lee's face. "So?" he said. "Hard for half-blind man to tell one bottle from another. Is bad?"

Thorson thought that over, and he remembered Hazzard lying dead in the *Trumpet* office and the man who'd pretended to be Huntley Drew putting his arms around Ginny to comfort her; and he remembered that man's speech in the darkness of Tom Conway's mine, the speech that had forged an organization which he'd intended to betray; and he remembered the whole vile parade of the man's pretense and villainy. "Not too bad, Quong," he said. "Considering the Sierraville raid and what it did to you, I guess you had the oldest claim on him. What was it you said about the mills of God grinding slowly yet exceeding small? Sometimes my own eyes don't see any too well. Probably I was mistaken about your using a different bottle that last time."

"Is good," said Quong Lee.

Thorson shrugged into his shirt and coat and went outside, and he found Ginny standing not many paces away, staring solemnly at the gulch that was shaping in the spreading dawn. She'd cried at Pi Hazzard's funeral, but she wasn't crying now. He came up behind her, putting his arms around her, and they stood this way in silence for a while. "They'll have to know the truth, those boys who went out with the gold and who'll be back again before many days," he said. "It will be better that way. I've given half-lies to men like Pat Shea and Zeke Lockhart who deserved honesty."

"We can have the paper tell them," she said. "There's wallpaper enough for another edition. And there must be an obituary for Belle, and the truth about her, too."

"The greatest vigilante of them all," he said.

They were silent again, until she spoke. "Last night you asked me to marry you, Tod. I see now why you did it. You were thinking that he was my father, and you were afraid of what the truth would do to me when it came out. You knew I'd need somebody to turn to, and you were going to be the one. I don't think I'll ever forget that, Tod."

"Belle was afraid for you," he said. "That's what gave me the courage to make my proposal then. But the idea wasn't new. Sometimes I think I had it from the first moment that I came into the *Trumpet* building and saw you. Has your answer changed?"

She turned, lifting her eyes to meet his, and when he saw the soul of her looking out at him, he knew that nothing had changed or ever would. "I remember one of the last things that Pi ever told me," she said. "When my chance at happiness came, I was to take it at once. Tod, oh, Tod!"

After a long while they broke free from each other, facing toward the camp again. Tod said, "Matthew Fee gave me a badge once. It wasn't worth the tin it was made out of, but I've kept it and now he's dead and the badge is good. And I'm remembering something Josh Hoskins told me the day I rode into Thunder Gulch, and I'm seeing the town as it will be when the gold bubble bursts. I'm seeing a railroad running over Wolverine Pass to take timber out of the hills and cattle out of the grassy valleys. Can you see it, Ginny?"

"Of course," she said. "I've always seen it."

Thus they stood sharing their vision and knowing that the reality of it was almost within their reach. And at long last they went into the gulch together, hand in hand and laughing, like little children going forth to greet the new and glorious day . . .